Feigning just slightly more fatigue than she actually felt, Loor dropped her staff a few inches. It was a subtle thing . . . but it gave the man an opening. He took it, darting forward and attempting to slam her in the face with his stick. Using exactly the same move he had used against her, she slipped to the side, thrust her stick between his knees, and levered his legs out from under him.

The man fell hard, his face twisting in a grimace of pain as he thudded to the ground. His stick flew from his hand.

Loor leaped onto him, standing on his right arm, her staff poised for a final strike. "Fall back!" she shouted. "Fall back—or he dies!"

But the men didn't move.

Loor glanced back down at the man on the ground. She expected to see his face full of fear and pain. But instead he was smiling. "Perfect!" he said.

Then two fingers on his right hand rose and fell. There was something practiced about it, as though it were a signal.

With that, every one of the tribesmen released their arrows. The air around her literally whistled as the shafts came at her from all sides.

I have failed, she thought. *But at least I have died honorably.*

And then the arrows hit.

PENDRAGON

BEFORE THE WAR

Book One of the Travelers
Book Two of the Travelers
Book Three of the Travelers

PENDRAGON
BEFORE THE WAR

BOOK THREE OF THE TRAVELERS

CREATED BY
D. J. MacHale

WRITTEN BY WALTER SORRELLS

Aladdin Paperbacks
New York   London   Toronto   Sydney

This book is a work of fiction. Any references to historical events, real people, or real locales are used fictitiously. Other names, characters, places, and incidents are the product of the author's imagination, and any resemblance to actual events or locales or persons, living or dead, is entirely coincidental.

ALADDIN PAPERBACKS
An imprint of Simon & Schuster
Children's Publishing Division
1230 Avenue of the Americas, New York, NY 10020
Copyright © 2009 by D. J. MacHale
All rights reserved, including the right of reproduction
in whole or in part in any form.
ALADDIN PAPERBACKS and related logo are registered
trademarks of Simon & Schuster, Inc.
The text of this book was set in Apollo MT.
Manufactured in the United States of America
First Aladdin Paperbacks edition March 2009
2 4 6 8 10 9 7 5 3 1
Library of Congress Control Number 2008929800
ISBN-13: 978-1-4169-6524-4
ISBN-10: 1-4169-6524-6

Contents

BOOK THREE OF THE TRAVELERS

LOOR

ONE

The sun was even stronger today.

Loor stood on the crest of the sand dune and looked into the distance. She had been following the thief for three days. She had never seen him though. The man she was following was a ghost, just a trail of indistinct footprints in the sand.

And when she had lost the trail, she had simply followed a huge bird—a hindor—that had been flying on the hot air currents above her since the moment she left Xhaxhu. A good luck charm or an actual guide—it was hard to say. But whatever the case, the great black bird had never steered her wrong.

But now she didn't really need the hindor. She could tell she was gaining on the thief because his footprints were becoming clearer. When she had first started tracking him at the outskirts of Xhaxhu, the prints had sometimes been nearly invisible, wiped away by the wind. In the beginning sometimes she'd had to backtrack, searching for the faintest sign of his passing. And sometimes he had played tricks on her, doubling back, jumping from rock to rock so as not to leave prints, leaving false trails. Anything to trip her up.

But not now. Now there was no losing the trail. It was just a contest of will. She shook her canteen. Will . . . and water. She had enough for another day if she stretched it. Another few hours if she didn't. Her lips were dry and cracked, and her feet were sore and blistered. Even with her dark, nearly black tone, the intensity of the sun had caused the skin on her shoulders and face to peel and burn.

Overhead the giant bird circled slowly, carried on the rising currents of hot air. The hindor was the only living creature she had seen in days. Not a snake, not a lizard, not a fly, or mosquito.

The desert was no place for people. The sky was a deep, clear blue, without even a hint of a cloud.

And then, for the first time, she saw him. There! The dunes rolled up and down in front of her. He was a small dark lump, three dunes away. He paused and looked back. He seemed to be in no hurry. She could tell that he saw her, though she couldn't see him in any detail. He wore the robes of the cannibal tribes of the desert. Beyond that, she could make out nothing.

He was watching her. Studying her. Looking for weakness. Finally he lifted his arm and gave her a silent, unhurried wave, as though acknowledging that she had made it this far.

Then he turned and disappeared.

She smiled fiercely.

Three days ago the desert had been the last thing on Loor's mind. It was the first day of Azhra, the biggest holiday of the year. Even hard-bitten warriors like Loor took time off from training during the weeklong festival. Everyone dressed in their finest clothes and ate their most delicious food. The streets of Xhaxhu were filled with color, and the city's fountains ran, just as they had in the old days.

There had been a time, years ago, when Xhaxhu lay at the center of an immense and fertile plain. Even though there was not much rainfall in the plains, great rivers ran through the land, irrigating the fields, and making the arid land bloom with life. The Festival of Azhra celebrated King Azhra, who brought his people through the desert to the watery and fertile oasis of Xhaxhu.

But over the years something changed. At first it was just a subtle decrease of the flow during the summer. Over time it became clear that something profound was happening. Some vast change in the weather was causing the rains in the distant mountains of Elzhe'er to cease for much of the year. And so the rivers dwindled and dried up.

Finally a neighboring people, the Rokador, created vast underground tunnels and aquifers, which would channel and store what little rain still fell in the distant mountains. The tunnels of the Rokador made it possible for farming to continue in much of the plains around Xhaxhu. But each year the Rokador reported sparser rains, fewer active streams, less water coming from the mountains of Elzehe'er.

And so, one after another, farms fell into ruin, orchards withered, fields were abandoned . . . and the sand blew ever closer to Xhaxhu.

But during the Festival of Azhra, all these things were forgotten. Loor's people, the Batu, forgot about the drought, and water flowed everywhere. Long ago the festival had signaled the beginning of the rainy season. The culmination of the festival was a great public ceremony in the central stadium of the city. There were speeches and dances and singing. Warriors paraded, showing off their skills and their finest uniforms.

And then, finally, a huge vessel of water was hoisted above the crowd. Each year a warrior took the ancient golden ax of Azhra and struck the vessel. It broke, dousing the crowd in water—symbolic of the life-giving rain that sustained the city.

This year Loor had been chosen for the honor of using the golden ax.

But on the first day of Azhra, an urgent message had summoned her to the Supreme Council, the body that advised King Khalek a Zinj, the king of Xhaxhu. Khalek had been in poor health lately, so his young son, Pelle a Zinj, was officially presiding. But because Pelle was still relatively inexperienced, he left most of the talking to his councillors. Loor's mother, Osa, was among those councillors, so Loor was not unfamiliar with the proceedings. But to have been called here, not as an observer, but as a participant—it was a great honor.

The news from the council had been grim. According to Chief Councillor Erran, the golden ax, which had been used for generations, had been stolen.

"Why would someone do that?" Loor said as she stood before the council.

One of the king's oldest councillors, Shakar, stood and pointed his finger across the room. "It is the Rokador!" he shouted. "Those traitors know the importance of Azhra to our people. They seek to humiliate us! We must strike against them now."

But Erran, the head of the council, rose and said, "Silence, Shakar! We do not know that it was the Rokador."

"Who else could it be?" Loor asked.

"We do not know, Loor." Loor's mother, Osa, stood and spoke. She looked much like Loor—tall, dark-skinned, strong. But her face was softer, and she smiled more easily. Today, however, she wasn't smiling. "Very likely the thief was a Zafir." The Zafir were fierce tribesmen who inhabited the deserts that surrounded Xhaxhu. "A man wearing the robes of a tribesman was spotted near the temple where the golden ax is stored."

"It could have been a Rokador dressed in desert robes!" shouted Shakar.

"Yes!" shouted another councillor. A loud hubbub erupted.

Erran raised his hands and silenced the room. "Let us not prematurely blame the Rokador," he said. "I have called Loor before us for a reason."

"What is that?" Loor said.

"The man in the robe was spotted in the outskirts of Xhaxhu not an hour ago. You are ordered to follow him into the desert. Follow him and retrieve the ax."

Loor turned to look at her mother. Osa looked back at her impassively. "Who should I take with me? Do I get to choose my team?"

Erran shook his head. "You will take no one. You will go alone."

Loor tried not to appear confused. Why would they send only her? Why not someone older? She studied her mother's face again. But Osa was showing nothing. An outside observer wouldn't have known from Osa's expression that she and Loor were even related.

For the first time Crown Prince Pelle a Zinj spoke. "If we send a large group, the group will go at the speed of its slowest member. No, Loor, your determination and resilience were well demonstrated in the games this year. You will go alone. You will find the thief. And you will take back what is rightfully ours."

When a Ghee warrior was given a direct order by a royal authority, there was no debate, no questioning. Ghee warriors simply did as they were told.

Loor knelt and pressed her forehead to the floor.

After the audience with the council, Osa accompanied her daughter back to her room.

"Why me?" Loor said finally. "There are many more experienced warriors in Xhaxhu. Did you get them to pick me?"

Osa shook her head. "You know I would not do that, Loor. It was Erran who suggested that you be the one. He felt your youth and vigor would be useful to the mission."

"Good," Loor said. "I would not want anyone to think I got the mission just because I was the great Osa's daughter."

Osa smiled. She put her hand on Loor's arm. "You earned the right to the assignment. Just do your duty and someday people will stop describing you as 'Osa's daughter.' In fact, they will probably be describing me as 'the great Loor's mother.'"

Loor almost laughed. But she didn't. Laughter was unbecoming of a serious warrior.

Thirty minutes later Loor's colorful holiday outfit lay in a pile on the floor of her room, and she was jogging into the western outskirts of the city, a heavy pack on her back, her war staff in her hand.

By midday she had found the thief's footprints. They wound through abandoned farms, and past dried out wells and twisted and leafless trees. And by the end of the day, she was into the sand. The thief's footprints were measured and unhurried. He showed no sign of fear, no sign of haste.

As she finally lay down on the sand, the stars twinkling above her, she was sure: This was no Rokador trick. There wasn't a Rokador in all of Zadaa who would march calmly into the desert like this. The Rokador word for the great desert was "shu-roka-nak." Loosely translated, it meant "the place where Rokador die."

No, the thief was a child of the desert.

She permitted herself a brief smile. The desert was unforgiving, and the tribesmen were tough and vicious. This would be a true test.

By the time the sun had neared the horizon, Loor had gained significantly on the thief. She had been pushing herself relentlessly. Even with all her arduous training, the desert was taking its toll on her. She had been forced to drink more water than she planned.

But it didn't matter. When she had first seen him, he was three dunes away. Now each time she crested a dune, she saw him struggling up the next dune.

She was close. Very close. But she had to catch him by nightfall. The thief almost certainly had more water than she did. If he slipped away during the night, she would run out of water once the sun began blazing on her the next morning. And without water, all her training, all her skill, all her will and determination were useless. She would die. It was that simple. She didn't have enough water to make it back to Xhaxhu.

She had dropped her pack hours earlier in order to make better time. Either she caught the thief, retrieved the ax, and took his water . . .

Or she died.

She was moving in a fog of pain now. Her feet burned, her lungs ached, her body was sore. And the lack of water was making her lose her edge. She began to entertain thoughts that she might die out here.

Her legs constantly threatened to give out under her.

And yet somehow she managed to go on. Still, relentlessly, she closed the gap.

As she crested the next dune, she saw that the landscape had changed. The dunes trailed off into a rocky, barren wasteland. Boulders and eerie rock formations thrust upward into the sky. She had heard of this place before. It was the high plateau that led to the mountains.

She could see the Elzehe'er range, white capped even at this time of year, rising in the distance.

Below her on the face of the last dune, she could see the man. For the first time he was hurrying, as though at long last he acknowledged her as a real threat. He looked back over his shoulder. He was slipping and sliding on the loose sand, trying to reach the sounder footing of the rocky plateau above them.

He was no more than a hundred yards away.

Loor felt a surge of pleasure. Yes. She was going to make it.

She paused, drained the last mouthful of water, tossed her canteen into the sand, then let out the shrill war cry of the Batu.

The echoes came back to her off the massive rock formations before her. In the distance the sun touched the top of one of the tall boulders. Then she saw the hindor pass in front of the red disk of the sun, its long black wings outstretched.

Loor raised her fighting staff and charged.

Two

Until this moment Loor had been unable to tell anything about the tribesman. Was he tall, short, pale, dark, muscular? There was no way to tell, given the massive scale of the dunes and the all-concealing folds of his robe.

But as she closed the gap, she saw that he was smaller than she'd expected. As a result he couldn't begin to match her speed. And, for the first time since she'd entered the desert, she was glad to be wearing the tiny outfit of a Ghee warrior instead of the bulky robe of the tribesman.

The thief didn't look back, though. He simply charged into the thicket of boulders, dodging this way and that. Loor was faster but the man was quick. Loor's legs were burning and her chest was on fire.

When she was only about fifty paces away, the man ducked between two stone pillars. She followed and found that he had entered a sort of stone chamber—a dead end surrounded by high walls of pale rock. Throughout the chamber were oddly shaped piles of rock, dozens of them, made from pieces about the size of her fist. They must have been man-made, though she couldn't think what they were for. Was it some sort of tribal burial ground? A religious site for the desert people?

The thief, still running, glanced back at her. He had nearly reached the end of the chamber. As he looked back, he tripped, sprawling on the hard rock.

Loor ran toward him. The thief lay with his back against the wall. As she approached, he looked up at her. Now she was able to clearly see his face. She was shocked at what she saw.

It wasn't a man at all.

It was just a boy, not more than eleven or twelve years old.

She halted and stared down at him. "Give me the ax," she said.

The boy said nothing.

"You led me on a good chase, boy," she said. "I applaud you. You are strong and brave. But I'm more than you can handle. Give me the ax and enough water for three days' journey through the sands, and I won't hurt you." To punctuate her demand, she lifted her stick, ready to strike the boy if he attempted to fight.

Still the boy said nothing. But a small grin ran across his face.

Suddenly Loor felt the hair stand up on the back of her neck. Her warrior instincts told her something was wrong. But it wasn't until she heard the sound that she knew what it was. The sound of rock scraping on rock.

A flood of anger ran through her.

She whipped around. Throughout the chamber the strange piles of rock began to move. Men rose from piles, like mythical creatures growing from the living rock.

But they weren't mythical creatures. They were desert tribesmen, carrying the distinctive short recurved bows of their people. Every bow was strung with an arrow.

Finally the last of them appeared, and the last rock fell away, clattering to the ground. For a moment there was no sound but the hot desert wind whistling softly across the top of the canyon.

Loor knew she had no chance against them. There must have been close to twenty men, hoods up, faces invisible. Every bow was trained on her. It was known that the desert tribesmen were masters of the bow. Having no crops in the desert, they sometimes had to survive for months on end on just the animals they shot.

But Loor had no intention of surrendering. She had been sent on a special mission by the crown prince himself. The only thing that would redeem her failure would be to die a good death.

"Give me the ax," she said again to the boy.

The boy pulled the ax from a fold beneath his robe. Loor felt a tug of excitement at the sight of it. The ancient wooden handle was intricately carved, displaying an artistic skill that she knew had been lost by her people long ago. The ax head itself was pure gold. Unlike the highly decorated handle, the ax head was simple—a battered wedge of metal, unmarked by anything other than the many blows it had struck over the years during the Festival of Azhra.

The boy threw it negligently on the ground.

As he did, a man detached himself from the group of

archers and walked haughtily toward her. "You think we care about such things?" he said.

"That ax is of great value," Loor said.

"It is dull and useless. A toy. If I wanted such a thing, it would be made of steel."

"Then I will take it," Loor said. "Just give me some water and I'll be on my—"

Before her hand could reach the ax, an arrow zinged through the air, hitting the ground only inches from the blade.

"If you want the ax," the man said, "you must take it from us."

With that, Loor sprang into action. She grabbed the ax and hurled it at the man who had been speaking. The man ducked fluidly, and the ax thudded into the head of one of the men behind him.

The man who had been talking slid the hood of his robe back smoothly. He was fair skinned—though not as fair as a Rokador—and dark haired. A thick scar split his face from one side to the other, and his left eye was just a puckered socket surrounded by scar tissue.

Loor charged him.

She expected a volley of arrows to follow. But instead the tribesmen simply followed her with their bows.

Before she could reach him, the one-eyed man had drawn a long, thin stick from beneath his robe. It was made from some kind of wood that she didn't recognize— gleaming, dense, and black. By the time she got to him, he was in a ready stance.

She didn't give him a chance to compose himself though. She simply attacked. The man's stick was much thinner than her own staff, so it moved more quickly. Loor had practiced stick fighting since she was old enough to hold a staff, but the man's techniques were unexpected. She was stronger and faster . . . but he seemed to have an answer for every attack she made.

"Son!" he called out to the boy on the ground. "What is our first rule of combat?"

"Never make the first move," the boy called back.

Loor tried to use the man's conversation to find an opening. But instead the man parried and hit her on her biceps. It wasn't enough to break her arm. But for a moment her limb went numb, and she thought she might lose the stick.

"You charged into this canyon without adequately studying it," the man said.

Loor felt sure that under normal circumstances she could have beaten the man fairly quickly. But she was feeling light-headed from exhaustion, heat, and dehydration. Each time she saw an opening in the man's guard, her limbs were too slow to exploit it.

Again the man hit her. His thin stick didn't seem to be intended to break bones, but only to cause pain. This made Loor mad. It wasn't even a real weapon. One blow from her stick could have ended the fight. But she just couldn't seem to land it!

Still, she relentlessly attacked, driving the man from one side of the canyon to the other. And still the arrows of the tribesmen followed her. Finally she saw another opening. Without breaking the rhythm of her attack, she dove forward.

Just at the moment she believed her stick would

impact with the man's head, though, he slipped to the side. His thin black stick whistled through the air, snaking between her legs. Using her own momentum against her, the man deftly levered her right leg out from under her and she crashed to the ground. She felt the skin tear on her knees.

But the pain was nothing. She had long ago ceased to think about pain.

"Never make the first move," the man said again, a broad smile briefly crossing his face.

Insults, on the other hand, still had the power to hurt her. She had been the finest stick fighter in Xhaxhu, her face put on posters, her skills talked about after every game. But this man was making a mockery of her.

With a scream she exploded to her feet. *I will not lose!* she thought. And this time, as she powered forward, the man fell back before her onslaught. With a surge of joy, she realized that she had started to understand his game. All his little feints and weight shifts and sly little darting movements wouldn't save him now. She understood him.

The man dodged and parried her hail of blows. From somewhere deep inside she summoned up the strength to make one last attack. But, she decided, it wasn't enough simply to win. She had to humiliate him.

Feigning just slightly more fatigue than she actually felt, she dropped her stick a few inches. It was a subtle thing . . . but it gave the man an opening. He took it, darting forward and attempting to slam her in the face with his stick. Using exactly the same move he had used against her, she slipped to the side, thrust her stick between his knees, and levered his legs out from under him.

The man fell hard, his face twisting in a grimace of pain as he thudded to the ground. His stick flew from his hand.

Loor leaped onto him, standing on his right arm, her staff poised for a final strike. "Fall back!" she shouted. "Fall back—or he dies!"

But the men didn't move.

Loor glanced back down at the man on the ground. She expected to see his face full of fear and pain. But instead he was smiling. "Perfect!" he said.

Then two fingers on his right hand rose and fell. There was something practiced about it, as though it were a signal.

With that, every one of the tribesmen released their arrows. The air around her literally whistled as the shafts came at her from all sides.

I have failed, she thought. *But at least I have died honorably.*

And then the arrows hit.

THREE

Loor expected pain.

But instead she felt only an odd sensation of constriction. And then she realized what had happened. The arrows they had fired had missed. All of them.

But it didn't matter. In a flash she knew the men hadn't meant to hit her in the first place. Every arrow they fired trailed a fine piece of rope. She was now surrounded by a web of rope. Around her the men were grabbing at the string and running in circles. She tried to struggle.

But by the time she had figured out what was going on, it was too late. Half the men ran in one direction, half in the other, their arms weaving rapidly as they passed one another. It was clear from the smoothness and coordination of their attack that this was a tactic they had practiced thousands of times before.

Within seconds she was completely enmeshed, circled from head to toe. The one-eyed man leaped deftly to his feet. Unable to move, she couldn't even resist as he pushed her to the ground and slid his long stick underneath the encircling mesh that bound her.

He studied her face. "Perfect," he said again. "Look at her. Even after three days in the desert, without enough water, she would have killed me." He smiled at his men. "You have done well, my men! King Allon will reward you greatly!" He snapped his fingers at two of the hooded men. "Take her."

The two men jumped forward and lifted the ends of the stick, hoisting Loor up onto their shoulders so that her head dangled above ground. With a feeling of horror Loor realized what must be happening. There were stories about the tribesmen. Stories of human sacrifice. Stories of cannibalism.

The only consolation she could find was that no one would ever know. Imagine the shame her mother would feel if she knew that Loor had been eaten by cannibals. A thing like that would stain the honor of a family for generations! She felt nauseated. Even the thought of her own death didn't sicken her as much as that.

"Before you have a chance to eat me," she said, "I'll starve myself. I'll make myself sick. I'll be foul tasting and diseased."

The one-eyed man laughed loudly. "Eat you!" he said. "You Batu are such idiots. I cannot believe you still tell those ridiculous stories. Our people have not eaten Batu in centuries."

"Then what do you want?" she said.

The man made a signal to his follows, a big circle in the air. Then he pointed to the entrance to the canyon. The men began walking single file. They carried her in front, like a trophy. Behind her she saw that the tribesmen had simply left the ax, the centuries-old treasure of her people, lying on the ground like discarded trash.

"The ax!" she said.

"It is of no consequence," the one-eyed man said. "It is just a useless bauble. In the desert everything must have a use. The desert is too unforgiving to allow for such frivolity."

Loor watched the ax disappear as the men slowly filed out of the canyon. Loor had always thought of herself as coming from the least frivolous people in the world. But she had to admit she could see the man's point. Out here, if you couldn't drink it or eat it or use it to keep the heat and cold from killing you, a thing was only going to drag you down.

"Where are we going?" she said.

"This is a great honor, you know," the man said.

Loor spit on the ground. Honor? This was the most demeaning thing that had ever happened to her in her life.

"We are a small, isolated people," the man said. "We need fresh blood to keep our people strong."

Loor blinked. What was he talking about?

"We knew that if we stole the ax, your king would send someone to recover it. A female warrior. Your men are strong, but Batu women can go farther and longer in the desert. So we knew that eventually a woman of unusual courage and fortitude would come to us." He smiled. "And here you are. Not only vital and strong . . . but young and beautiful."

"And you sent a ten-year-old boy to do this? Your own son? What if we had captured him? What if we had killed him? What if he had died in the desert?"

"Surely you understand the concept of honor," the man said, clapping his son gently on the shoulder. "And he is eleven."

The boy looked so proud that he was about to burst.

Loor had to admire these people. They were not quite what she expected.

The one-eyed man smiled fondly at his son. "What a story he will have to tell his grandchildren! 'At the age of eleven, I broke into the great city of Xhaxhu and stole their greatest treasure.' A price cannot be put on a thing like that."

"You still have not answered my question," Loor said. "What precisely do you want from me?"

"King Allon," he said, "has reached a certain point in his life. The time has come to have an heir to the throne."

"What are you *talking* about?" she demanded.

The line of men finished filing out of the rocks and started up the face of the first dune. They were heading back into the desert. In the distance she could see that the sun had slipped behind the horizon. The sky was a wash of brilliant pink. Already the air had begun to cool. Soon, she knew from experience, it would be quite cold.

"Quiet," he said softly. "We do not speak in the desert. Every time you open your mouth to speak, your breath exhales moisture. To speak in this place is to squander precious water on the lifeless sand."

"I will stop talking when you answer my question!" Loor howled. "What are you doing with me?"

The one-eyed man studied her as though considering

whether he should waste any of his body's precious water on her.

"Congratulations," he said finally. "In three days you will marry the king of the Zafir."

Then the one-eyed man put up his hood, and his face disappeared into the darkness.

FOUR

For the next day and a half not a single man spoke. They walked slowly through the sand, not wasting a single step or a single motion.

Around midday the next day, they left the shifting sands again and began winding through a series of barren foothills in the shadow of the Elzehe'er range, slowly climbing higher and higher. The air began to cool somewhat, but the land was still parched and arid.

Late in the day they crested a small rocky outcrop. And suddenly, spread out in a small valley below them was an astonishing sight.

Water.

Not just a little water, but a vast lake of it. Surrounding the lake was a green valley. Flocks of sheep gamboled across the grass. And in the distance, perhaps a mile away on the shore of the lake, lay a broad colorful maze of tents. There were red tents, yellow tents, white tents, orange tents, tents made from several colors, tents painted with designs. It was a riot of color.

As they crested the hill and spotted the tent city

below them, the men all dropped their hoods and cheered. Then they placed Loor on the ground and cut her free from the web that secured her to the stick.

Loor's first instinct was to try to escape. But after being tied to a pole and fed almost nothing for a solid day, she could barely stand. Her feet were asleep, her muscles felt rubbery, and she felt dizzy and slow witted.

The men sat in a circle around her and laid out a meal. Loor hated to admit it, but it smelled better than any food she'd ever experienced. There were smoked meats and fish, dried fruits, spiced pickles.

Loor considered not eating for a moment, just to spite them. But then she realized that if she was going to escape, she needed to get her strength back. She ate slowly, resisting the impulse to shove all the food into her mouth.

When they were done, the one-eyed man put his hand over his heart—the standard greeting of the desert people—and said, "I am Heshar. I am proud to know you."

Loor glared at him. "Loor," she said, patting her own chest. "I will be proud to kill you one day."

Heshar smiled as though she had just given him a high compliment. "Come," he said. "Let us take you to the king."

As she stood, a shadow slid across the grass in front of her. She looked up. High above her the hindor circled slowly on the breeze.

She was amazed that it had followed her this far.

Good luck is still with me, she thought. *Perhaps I can still complete my mission.*

In Xhaxhu important people lived in large stone buildings that oozed a sense of power and authority. But the king of the Zafir lived little differently from his people. His tent was a bit larger and had a brilliant red pennant hanging from its high center pole. But otherwise it was distinguishable from the living quarters of others only by the hard-faced guards who stood outside the entry flap, eyes restlessly scanning the horizon.

As they approached, the guards put their hands over their hearts and greeted Heshar solemnly. He seemed to be a respected man here.

"Is this her?" a white-haired man with a large mustache asked.

Heshar nodded. The guards studied her with undisguised interest. All the women in the camp were clothed from head to toe in robes. By comparison Loor seemed nearly naked. But Loor felt that she was being studied more the way one would study a livestock specimen than a woman.

The white-haired man nodded. "You have done well, Heshar."

Then he snapped his fingers at one of the guards. The guard disappeared into the tent. Finally he returned with a carefully folded robe of fine silk. Loor could smell the perfume wafting off of it.

"Cover yourself," the white-haired man said.

Loor threw the beautiful robe on the ground. "I am Batu," she said. "Robes slow you down, weaken your ability to fight."

The white-haired man eyed her silently for a while.

"As you wish," he said. Then he pulled back the flap of the tent and motioned her to enter.

Loor was a little shocked. She was still wearing her dagger on her hip. No Batu guard would ever have allowed an armed stranger to approach a Batu leader.

She walked inside, followed by Heshar.

The tent was large and brightly lit, the sunlight entering through a series of cleverly designed vents in the roof. Three musicians sat near the door, playing quietly on stringed instruments. A light haze of smoke filled the room.

At the far end of the tent sat a man in a perfectly white robe. Flanking him were ten men, short spears cradled in their laps.

"Please," the man said. "Sit."

She walked up until she was about ten feet from the man. Was this the king? She wasn't sure. He was slim, with a handsome face, and bright black eyes. Loor estimated that he was maybe five years older than she was—perhaps twenty. He wore no signs of rank—no crown, no jewelry, no fancy sword, no ornaments at all.

"I will not sit," she said.

The man shrugged. "What is your name?"

"Loor."

"I am Allon. It is my privilege to rule the Zafir."

Loor crossed her arms over her chest and didn't speak.

"Have you been mistreated?" King Allon said.

"If you mean have I been taken and dragged here against my will, yes. I was not beaten."

The king laughed. "Oh, Heshar, Heshar," he said to

the one-eyed man. "I am well pleased with your work." He turned to the men flanking him. "Look at her! Is she not magnificent? Such spirit! Such inner strength!"

The men nodded soberly. Everyone seemed relaxed and complacent.

Loor chose that moment to grab her dagger and hurl herself at the king. Before she could reach him, however, his men had grabbed their spears and leaped to their feet. They were blindingly fast.

One of the men grabbed her by the waist and wrestled her to the floor. He made a move as if to punch her in the face. But the king said, "No, no." His voice was gentle. But there was authority beneath the soft tone. Loor had to admit she was impressed.

The man who'd tackled her raised his hands and stepped off her.

"I presume," King Allon said, "that my friend Heshar has told you why you were brought here."

She laughed. "I'll die before I submit to you."

The king raised one eyebrow. "You could have thrown yourself on that spear point," he said. "But you didn't."

Loor gnashed her teeth. He had a point. As a rule, Loor disliked clever people. "The time was not right," she said.

"Mm . . ." The king seemed unpersuaded. "Among my people pointless death is not considered honorable. If one is going to give one's life, it ought to be for a purpose."

Loor didn't answer. One could talk all day about such things and never come to any conclusions. Battle was the only place where anything was really ever solved.

The king rose. "Come," he said. "Join me."

He walked toward the door. Having nothing better to do, Loor followed him. Clearly now was not the time to attack this man. She would bide her time, wait for the right moment. Then she would strike.

Like all the other Zafir she had seen so far, the king moved with a slow, graceful stride, not wasting any energy. It was quite different from Xhaxhu, where everyone was expected to move quickly and decisively at all times. To the Batu, slow movement was a sign of weakness.

As the king walked past his subjects, they placed their hands over their hearts. But there were no bowed heads, no obvious signs of subservience. And the king returned their greetings as though they were friends.

It didn't take long to reach the outskirts of the tent city. As they did, King Allon turned to his guards and said, "Leave us."

The men nodded. King Allon walked on, heading slowly toward the shore of the immense lake.

"You must have great confidence in your skills as a fighter," she said.

"Oh?"

"Well, I am one of the most dangerous warriors in Xhaxhu. If you think you can best me in one-armed combat . . ." She shrugged.

The king smiled. "In the long run," he said, "I cannot very well have a queen whom I fear. At a certain point, I simply have to trust you."

Loor was astonished. She suspected a trick. Maybe he had some kind of dangerous weapon hidden in his robe. "Then you are a fool," she snapped.

"Mm . . ." He trailed off.

"Each summer for a thousand generations my people have come to this lake to fatten our sheep. During fall, winter, and spring we are scattered like seeds across the whole desert. We are a fierce and warlike people. During the rest of the year, the various tribes that make up my nation are in constant war with one another. They engage in feuds that go back generations. But here? This is called the 'Lake of Peace.' For the three months we are here, there are no quarrels, no fights, no voices raised in anger. To break that law is to die on the spot. No matter what the cause or provocation."

"Why?" Loor said.

"This." The king stopped and made a sweeping gesture with his hands, encompassing the huge lake. Loor looked out at the water. It was impossibly blue. She had never seen so much water, not in her entire life. She amazed to find that she could actually smell it. "If we, as a people, are to survive the hot months," King Allon said, "we must fatten our sheep. Our sheep are our lifeblood. We eat their flesh and weave out clothes and tents from their wool. This place is our source. If war and hatred and fear and vengeance are allowed to enter this valley, we all will suffer. In the end we all will starve, and our people will vanish from the earth. So . . . here peace reigns."

"We have an arrangement much like that," Loor said.

"The Batu and the Rokador do not like each other very much. But they provide us with water. And we provide them with food and protection."

The king surveyed the land. As he did, he spotted the hindor flying in the distance. "That is a great omen," he said. "Among our people, the hindor is considered the greatest of birds."

"Yes," she said. "We too prize it for its fierceness and strength."

"That is not why we revere it," the king said. "We worship the hindor because it can smell water from miles and miles away. Follow a hindor's flight, and eventually you will reach water."

"That one followed me all the way here," Loor said.

King Allon's eyebrows went up. "All the way across the desert?"

She nodded.

"Astonishing." He smiled. "You will bring us great fortune."

Loor said nothing. The king picked up a rock, skipped it across the water. It must have skipped seven or eight times. "Try it," he said.

She picked up a rock from the bank, threw it in the water. It went *plooop!* and sank immediately.

"No," he said. "Like this." He showed her the way he threw it.

She tried it. The stone skipped twice and sank. "Yes!" the king said. "You see!" He smiled, apparently happy as a child. "I used to do this all the time when we came here in the summer. I'd herd my father's flock way off over there. Then I would throw stones for hours!"

He threw another one, then clapped his hands joyously. "Only six that time," he said.

"I will beat you," she said. She picked up a rock and hurled it as hard as she could. Two skips and a violent splash.

He laughed again. "Not so hard. Gently!" He searched for a stone until he found one he liked. On this throw it skipped so many times she couldn't even count them. The king seemed to find this hilarious.

Loor tried to envision old King Khalek a Zinj doing something like this. It was impossible even to imagine. A thing like this was beneath his dignity.

She searched for a flat rock like the one he'd used. She tried her best to imitate the low arc he used in throwing his stones. This time her rock seemed to dance across the water. It only made about four skips. But still. "Yes!" she shouted, raising her hands above her head.

"Good! Good!" the king shouted. Then he put his arm around her shoulder and gave her a quick hug. It seemed a simple and genuine—almost brotherly—acknowledgment of her accomplishment in this little game. But she could feel his muscles beneath the robe. He was stronger than he looked.

Loor felt a strange glow spread through her. It took her a moment to realize what it was. She *liked* this man. A lot.

A terrible thought ran through her mind. She had no way of getting back across the desert. She had no friends here. And this man, whom she was beginning to like, wanted her to stay forever. A frightening notion—and it was only a notion—flitted through her mind. *What if I just gave in? What if I just stayed?*

Her entire life had been nothing but struggle. Training, fighting, striving, working—it was nothing but pain and sacrifice.

All along the banks of the great lake, she saw flocks of sheep munching peacefully on the grass. Shepherds sat around here and there, some by themselves, some laughing and joking in small groups. Small brooks babbled, pouring water into the lake.

In Batu mythology there was a paradise from which all humanity had originally come. In Loor's mind it looked exactly like this.

King Allon stood beside her still, his arm draped across her shoulder.

Loor froze. *What am I thinking?* she asked herself.

The next moment her blade was in her hand.

The young king twisted sharply—but not before her knife had entered the folds of his robe. And then his powerful hands clamped around hers. She was unable to move.

"Just because I throw stones into a lake does not mean I am a fool," he said softly. Then his face lit up with another mysterious smile. He pushed the knife back out of the fold of his robe. With a quick snap of his hands, he applied excruciating pain to her wrist. Her knife fell to the ground. He kicked it into the water.

Loor felt a torrent of shame run through her. He'd evaded her knife effortlessly. She'd punctured nothing but cloth. She was sure her aim had been perfect. It was not normal for Loor to feel helpless. But right now she felt completely helpless.

"I cannot be your friend," she said. "I cannot be your wife. I cannot be one of your people."

The king waved his hand as though none of this was very important. "We have a saying, 'There is much time in the desert.'"

"Which means what?"

"Things happen. Circumstances change. What seems right today may seem wrong tomorrow." He looked at the sun, which was starting to sink toward the horizon. "Are you hungry, Loor?"

"I suppose so."

"Let us go eat," he said.

They began walking silently toward the crimson pennant over his distant tent.

"Where does all the water go?" she asked as they approached the cluster of brightly colored tents.

"From the lake, you mean?" he said.

She pointed around the margins of the lake. "I see all this water coming in. But there's no river going out."

"They say that once there was a river," King Allon said. "But then one day it just stopped flowing. Like that." He snapped his fingers, then shrugged. "The world is full of mysteries."

They walked silently.

When they had finally reached their tent, the young king stopped and turned to her. "We are free people," he said. "I will not keep you here against your will."

"Then I will leave right now," she said.

"I will not send anyone to escort you home, either,"

he said. He pointed toward the mountains, their peaks a fiery red as they reflected the blaze of the setting sun. "Those peaks rise twenty thousand feet into the air. To the north and south lies a plateau where there is not a tree or leaf or blade of grass. To the east, between here and Xhaxhu, is only desert sand. There are no maps but the ones in our heads." He tapped his temple. "If you leave this place, you will die." He stroked the side of her face. "And I will be very sad for you."

The king's retainers spotted them and began walking briskly toward them. "Your Highness!" one of them said, pointing at the king's midsection.

The king looked down at the large red stain that was spreading slowly down the front of his robe.

"It is nothing," King Allon said. "Send word to my cook to bring out the food. Loor and I will eat by the lake."

FIVE

It wasn't nothing though. By the time that Loor had finished eating, the red stain had grown to cover much of King Allon's lap. The young king's face was pale and drawn. It was obvious that his men were alarmed at all the blood. But none of them said a word about it. So she had been correct, her aim had been true. But this man, this kind man, was strong of both body and will.

In fact, King Allon continued to talk with her as though nothing at all had happened. His conversation was lively and interesting—tough, realistic, yet generous and wise. She had an odd realization: Batu boys bored her. They seemed so obvious, so loud, so tedious. Batu boys were always telling you how great they were, how strong, how fearless. But Allon, he hadn't talked about himself even for a second.

"Look," she said finally, waving at all the blood, "you have to do something about that. You will die if you keep bleeding."

"Is that not what you want?" he said.

Loor said nothing.

King Allon smiled his mysterious smile. "Well then, if you have eaten your fill, I think I might take a little rest."

That night Loor was left all alone in the tent. A simple woolen mat lay in the center for her to sleep on. Next to it was a woolen robe, as white and pure as the king's.

After the sun went down, Loor lay down on the mat and stared up at the tent roof. She could feel the robe lying there. The air had grown cold. She had nothing to wear but her Batu combat gear.

What if I just went ahead and put it on? she thought.

She couldn't sleep. All she could think about was the king, sitting there talking with her as his blood slowly drained onto the floor.

"Never make the first move." Wasn't that what the one-eyed man's son had said? She had made a move before she'd thought everything through. And now she was sorry.

Loor felt her eyes sting as she stared up into the air. She'd failed in her mission, failed in her attempt to kill her captor, failed in everything. Why hadn't they picked someone else to come out here? *I am too young,* she thought. *They should have chosen someone else.*

And then, suddenly, she knew what she needed to do. It was time to stop feeling sorry for herself. She stood, pulled the robe over body, let it slip down over her bare skin. It was an odd sensation. She wasn't used to wearing things like this.

Then she gathered what she would need and walked out of the tent, continuing past the other silent tents.

A dog barked, then went quiet. She walked toward the lake. A thin wedge of moon illuminated it. The surface was still and black. Today it had looked beautiful. Now it looked terrifying, like some dark force that might suck her down and destroy her.

Hesitantly she approached the lake. Loor knelt and looked down. She could see her face reflected in the dark water. Only her eyes were visible.

Finally she leaned over and drank, drank until her belly was full. Then she stood and waded into the water.

It was so frigid that she gasped. She had never been in water before, nothing deeper than a two-inch-deep bath. She had heard the Rokador actually had pools that they swam in. But water was too precious in Xhaxhu for such frivolous use.

A band of fear closed around her chest. But she forced herself to walk out farther into the water. She could feel the pebbles shifting under her feet. Deeper and deeper she went, her heart pounding as the cold black water surrounded her. With each step she grew more frightened. She had not been frightened at all when she had been fighting for her life the other day. But this—this was terrifying.

She was up to her neck in the water. A few more strides and she would sink beneath the water and drown.

She took a deep breath. And waited.

"There is much time in the desert," she said, speaking the words out loud. "There is much time in the desert. There is much time in the desert."

And then she felt something strange around her, something moving inside her robe.

She smiled. Yes! It was working!

Every Zafir robe was constructed with tiny bladders of a substance that absorbed water. Any water that came in contact with it would be filtered and sucked into the bladders, where it would remain until you opened them to drink.

It was these ingeniously constructed robes that allowed the Zafir to move through the desert for days on end without dying of thirst.

Loor walked slowly out of the water. The robe was amazingly heavy now that it was full of water. *No wonder the Zafir walk so slowly,* she thought. *This is heavy as lead!*

An hour later she was walking into the dark, silent dunes.

Six

Loor was not the sort of person to doubt herself. But now that she was out in the desert, she realized how foolish she had been. Xhaxhu was to the east of the Elzehe'er Mountains. But simply plodding toward the rising sun was no way to get through hundreds of miles of shifting sand. There were no landmarks, no roads, no signs—nothing to indicate precisely where to go. Compared to the massive desert, the mighty city of Xhaxhu was just a speck on the map. She could easily miss it and wander right on into the deserts to the west of the city.

Plus, the robe with its pockets full of water was heavy and hot. Even though she knew that it helped her conserve water and guarded her skin from the sun, it still felt constricting and awkward. She knew that her progress was much slower than it would have been without the robe.

By noon on the first day, she was feeling light-headed from the heat. With the heavy robe around her, her body built up heat unmercifully.

Loor was a strong girl. Years of grueling training

had toughened her mind and body. But one of the things you learned through years of hard physical labor was that every body, no matter how hard it had been trained, had limits. When you crossed those limits, the machine broke down. The toll of three days in the desert had robbed her body of fluids and minerals that one evening of eating and drinking had not quite replenished.

It wasn't her body that seemed to be taking it the hardest, though. She knew she could push her body further. She had water and a little food that she'd brought with her. But her mind just didn't feel sharp.

She found herself fixating on things in the distance, imagining things on the horizon, staggering toward them without thinking. One time she realized she had gone for hours without thinking anything at all. And as she did so, her path had started curving off in the wrong direction. North. She looked back and saw her tracks in the sand. She'd been walking north instead of east for what might have been several miles. And she hadn't even known it!

Concentrate! Loor told herself. But still, her mind felt fuzzy and weak.

She started seeing things that weren't there. People on the horizon. Trees. An oasis. They were all mirages—just figments of her imagination. With nothing to see but sand and empty sky, her mind was putting things out there that didn't exist.

And this was only the first day! What would it be like by the third or fourth day, when she started running low on water?

But there was nothing she could do now. She could only plod on and hope for the best.

Eventually the sun got so high in the sky that she couldn't tell what was east and what was west based on the sun. She decided to stop, rest, and eat.

She pulled the rubber tube out of the neck of the robe and sucked on it. To her surprise the tube simply gurgled. No water came out. She knew the robe was capable of holding several days' worth of water, so it was obviously a problem with the tube. She checked it for leaks. Nothing. She sat on the hot sand and squeezed the robe. This forced water up into the tube. She drank deeply. It was hot, but pure. She sighed with contentment and nibbled on the dried lamb she'd brought with her.

A wave of exhaustion poured over her as she sat. She knew that conserving her strength was as important as conserving her water. Deciding that a nap might be a good idea, Loor bunched up her hood to form a pillow, lay down in a ball, and fell asleep.

When she woke up, Loor felt much better. She was a little surprised at how long she'd slept, though. The sun was heading down toward the horizon.

She stretched and sighed. She felt a *lot* better! Stronger, lighter, cooler. She stood. Maybe it was her imagination, but the robe itself seemed lighter.

Suddenly she had the oddest sensation—as though she were not alone. She whipped around, assuming a fighting stance, ready for anything. Then she laughed.

The hindor.

The big black bird was perched at the top of the

dune on which she was standing, looking down at her with its large yellow eyes.

"Hello, bird!" she called. "Are you going to bring me luck?"

The bird, of course, just stared at her.

Loor didn't think of herself as the sort of person to talk to birds. But out here? It no longer seemed to matter. "Are you going to lead me home?" she called.

The bird stared at her for another moment or two, then disappeared over the dune. She was sorry to see it go. But then it glided smoothly back around in a slow arc, passing over her head and winging to the east.

She decided to follow.

Hindors led you to water—was that not what King Allon said? If the desert tribesmen believed it to be true, it probably was. Since the only water to the east was in Xhaxhu . . . well, that had to be where the hindor was heading.

As the hindor soared east, she began walking. Her legs felt stronger, she was cooler, and she felt as if she were twenty pounds lighter. Her mood brightened.

Even though she might not actually have the ax in her possession, she knew where it was. It would be easy enough to lead an expedition out and claim it, once she found her way back to Xhaxhu.

She kept her eyes pinned on the slow-flying hindor as she swiftly walked on. After a few minutes she pulled the rubber hose out of the robe and took another sip. Again it gurgled. She bunched the robe up again to push more water to the hose. But still it gurgled.

As she was standing there, she felt something on

her leg. A tickling sensation, like an ant crawling on her skin.

But she knew there were no ants out here. She looked down curiously. It wasn't an ant, but a bead of water running slowly down her leg. Sweat? Maybe.

Then she noticed something in the sand. A small round stain near her foot. A water drop. She snapped her head around and looked behind her. Parallel to her footprints in the sand were a series of little round stains.

The robe's water-storage system had a leak in it. She had been dumping water, drip by drip by drip, for twelve solid hours. No wonder the robe felt so light! As she slept, she'd been draining all her water into the sand!

Had King Allon intentionally given her a leaky robe? Or had she punctured it somehow as she slept. There was no way to know.

But it didn't matter. The fact was, she was almost out of water.

She looked back toward the mountains. She estimated that the sun would be setting in about an hour. Once the sun went down, water wouldn't be a problem. She could easily keep walking all night without replenishing. But then once the sun rose, the heat would begin pulling the water out of her. She'd have a few hours, and then the well-tuned machine that was her body would fail.

And that would be that.

She had a decision to make. If she turned around right now and headed straight back toward the mountains, she *might* be able to find the valley where King Allon was. And she'd survive. She'd survive as the slave of a barbarian king.

Or she could press on. And probably die.

There was no time to waste. She had to decide.

She took a deep breath. Last year she had run in the Pizon, the great fifty-mile footrace that was run every three years in Xhaxhu, where all the best warriors competed to show off their endurance. She'd come in fourth, a great showing for a girl her age. Fifty miles in less than eight hours. Would fifty miles get her to Xhaxhu?

It might.

Of course, during the Pizon she'd had water breaks. How much water had she drunk during the race? Gallons probably.

Well. There was no choice was there? Not really. Not when you were a Ghee warrior. Death or slavery? That was easy.

She spent the next ten minutes squeezing every last drop out of the robe. She was amazed at how much was still there.

To the east the hindor was tracing a lazy circle in the air. As if it were waiting for her.

"Here I come!" she shouted.

She dropped the empty robe on the ground. And then she began to run.

SEVEN

The moon rose early, dusting the dunes with a dim silver light. It wasn't bright. But it was enough.

Loor ran without stopping. She'd run the Pizon on a flat surface, with shoes made for running. Now she was running on loose sand. Every stride took more effort. Climbing the face of a dune was a monumental struggle. Then once she started running down the other side of the dune, she had to be careful not to fall.

Above her, the stars were so bright that she could make out the black shape of the hindor as it blotted them out, one after another, in its slow path through the sky.

Soon Loor's world had narrowed to only a few things—the dark shape of the hindor, the silver-flecked sand, and the pain. Pain in her muscles. Pain in her lungs. Pain in her feet as her shoes blistered her heels and toes.

She ran on and on and on and on.

Eventually she grew thirsty. Even in the coolness of the night, running for hours on end drove the water from her pores as surely as the sun did.

Soon the thirst began to blot out the other pain, just as the hindor blotted out the stars. Still she willed herself on.

Follow the hindor, she repeated. *Follow the hindor. Follow the hindor.*

Soon it became a rhythm, merging with the sound of her footfalls in the sand, with the steady intake of her breath, with the beating of her heart.

And slowly, stride by stride, her strength began to ebb away.

Strangely, though, as her body began to fail, she felt an odd joy rising in her. It was as though she had separated from her body. Some part of her mind left the pain and exhaustion behind and floated up above her, light and buoyant as the hindor.

This was the way to die, she thought. Driven to the utmost extremity of pain and fear and weakness. No one could say she had failed! She had done everything she could.

As the sun began to paint the distant horizon with a wash of pink, she slowed to a walk. It wasn't a choice. There was no running left in her. Her tongue was stuck to the roof of her mouth. Her legs were chafed raw. Her feet were a ruin of blisters.

The sun began to rise. And still the hindor flew east. And still she staggered on.

There was no sign of Xhaxhu. Not a dried-up well. Not a fallen tree. Nothing but sand.

And then the hindor began to drift down from the sky. At first she thought it was her imagination. But it was not. The hindor was coming down, down. Eventually it landed.

Loor's vision had gotten blurry. It seemed as though the hindor was perched on something. A rock maybe, sticking up out of the sand. It seemed a very long way away.

She tripped and fell.

Maybe I should just lie here, she thought. *Maybe I should just rest.*

The hindor sat motionless on its perch, staring at her. Waiting.

Loor stared at the bird. The bird stared back. And then she came to a sudden realization. Hindors were scavengers. They fed off the carcasses of the dead.

She began to laugh.

Water? The hindor wasn't looking for water! It was just waiting for her to die. It had sensed the truth days ago: This odd creature, this human, was a stranger in the desert. This creature was doomed from the start.

Loor sat up. The laughter hurt her parched throat. But still she couldn't stop. All this time she'd been thinking this huge black bird was good luck. How wrong she'd been!

She forced herself to her feet. "You are not getting my bones." She had intended it to be a yell, a war cry. But it came out as a hoarse, pathetic croak.

She fell, and began to crawl toward the bird. She would strangle it, she decided. Or beat its head against the oddly shaped rock on which it was perched.

"We will die together, bird," she whispered. She crawled closer and closer, every inch a struggle. Still the bird didn't move.

She could feel the heat of the sun beating on her,

sucking the last moisture from her skin. She had stopped sweating a long time ago. A bad sign. But it didn't matter. She was going to take the bird with her.

And then, just as she reached the rock, the bird flapped its wings. Once. Twice. And then it rose lazily into the air.

She pressed her forehead against the rock. It was strangely cool. It had a strange smell, too. What was it? Then she remembered. It was the smell of the Lake of Peace. The smell of water.

There was a soft vibration in the stone. And she could hear something now—the sound of rushing water.

She frowned. It was a hallucination of course. There was no water here.

There was something odd about the stone, though. It seemed more like concrete than stone. She pushed herself to her feet and stared over the lip of the rock.

It was perfectly circular. Her heart jumped. Whatever this was, it wasn't natural. It was man-made. In fact, it looked like something made by the Rokador.

She heaved on the stone lid with the last of her strength. It slid off, revealing a hole. A hole that went down into darkness.

But the sound that came from the hole was unmistakable. It was the sound of rushing water.

Astonished and completely out of strength, Loor sagged over the side and reached down. The water was too far away.

Imagine, she thought vaguely, if she died here not more than an arm's length from water. She reached down farther and farther, until finally she was balanced precariously on the edge. Her head was spinning and her ears rang. It was hard to maintain her balance.

Then she slipped.

Headfirst Loor plunged down into the darkness.

Eight

People who live in the middle of deserts rarely know how to swim. Loor was no exception.

She fell headlong into a torrent of water that spun her and thrashed her like a doll. Water went up her nose, into her lungs, into her stomach. With what little energy she had, she flailed helplessly at the water as she was sucked along through the darkness. She tried to hold her breath.

Suddenly, as she started to lose consciousness, the water slowed a little, and she hit something hard. She pulled herself forward, found herself on a flat surface of rock. Her toes and fingers trailed in the water. She moved her head until her lips were touching the water, then took a few sips. And with that, she collapsed.

How long she lay in the cool darkness, she couldn't say. It seemed like a long time. Every now and then she gained enough strength to take a few more sips of water. Then she would lose consciousness again.

Eventually, though, the water revived her. She was able to sit up. *Bam!* Her head smacked into solid rock, and she saw stars.

Carefully she crawled along the rock. She found herself on a sort of ledge, just inches from the running water. As best she could tell, she was in some sort of giant pipe. It had to be the work of the Rokador. But where it came from or where it led, she had no idea. She couldn't see anything at all.

So she just kept crawling.

Eventually she saw a tiny point of dim light in the distance. She crawled toward it. Gradually it took the form of an arch at the far end of the pipe she was crawling through. Her knees were getting cut and bruised from all the crawling, but since she couldn't swim, there was no other way to reach the light.

Eventually she crawled out of the tunnel, through the stone arch, and into an immense chamber. It was more than just a room full of water. It was an underground lake.

The illumination came from a small artificial light source on the wall. It lit the area immediately around it, and then faded into a distant gloomy darkness. The chamber was so large she couldn't see where it ended.

"Hello!" Loor called. Her voice was only a soft croak. But it echoed and re-echoed again and again in the huge underground chamber. She cleared her throat. "Anybody here?" Her voice was stronger now.

There was no answer.

The ledge she was on had widened out at the tunnel's end. She stood and walked unsteadily until she was standing under the light. A small door was cut into the rock. On it was a sign that read DO NOT PASS.

She tried the door, but it was locked. She banged furiously. No one answered.

How far was she from Xhaxhu? For all she knew, she could still be fifty miles away. Even if she knew how to swim, it would be too far for her to swim in her weakened state. And since she did not know how to swim? There seemed no chance.

That was when she noticed the boat.

She had never actually *seen* a boat. But she had read about them. A boat was a thing that allowed you to float on water. This was a small wooden thing, not much longer than she was tall, tied to the edge of the ledge. It was dirty and looked as if it hadn't been used in years.

What choice did she have? She stepped into the boat.

To her surprise the boat moved rapidly from side to side when she put her weight on it, wobbling wildly. She fell hard, smacking into the bottom of the tiny craft.

When she finally managed to sit up, she saw that she had knocked the rope free. The little boat was drifting, slowly, slowly, slowly, away from the dock.

How do you make it move? she wondered. *How do you control it?*

She had no idea. She had seen in books that people used flat sticklike things with handles, dipping them in the water and pushing the boat around somehow. But this boat had no such device in it. In fact, it had nothing in it.

Loor felt a momentary stab of terror. The boat wobbled every time she moved. It was drifting out into the darkness, heading . . . where? She didn't know. And if the boat tipped over, she'd fall into the black water and drown.

So she lay down, reached into her pocket, and pulled out the last soggy piece of dried lamb. Just the effort of chewing it made her feel tired. But the sweet taste of the lamb restored some of her determination. In a minute she'd figure out a way of moving the boat around, and then . . .

She noticed the boat was moving a little faster now. She was bobbing along, deep in the darkness of the underground lake, far from the small light. It seemed as if the boat were being sucked along now. Then she heard a distant rushing noise.

She huddled in the bottom of the boat. Something was happening. And she was powerless to do anything about it.

Suddenly the craft was moving faster and faster. And then the rushing noise was all around her. She couldn't see, but she could tell by the compressed sound that she was inside a tunnel again.

The water grew rougher and faster. She clung to the boat with all her strength.

I hate *water!* she thought. *I hate it!*

The boat slammed and banged and thumped and rocked and bumped. It was about the most frightening thing she'd ever done, right up there with wading out into the Lake of Peace. Worse, actually, because she couldn't turn back, couldn't control the boat, couldn't do anything but hang on and try not to scream.

It seemed to go on for hours.

And then suddenly the rushing noise became a roar, and the roar became thunder, and the boat went faster and faster.

And then she was flying through the darkness.

When she hit, she lost consciousness.

Nine

How long have I been here?" Loor asked, looking up from the bed where she was lying. Chief Councillor Erran stood over her. Loor saw her mother, Osa, seated at the foot of the bed.

"Four days," Erran said. "We thought we were going to lose you. A farmer found you lying in an irrigation ditch on the outskirts of the city. Where have you been?"

Loor sighed loudly. "I failed," she said.

Erran and Osa exchanged glances. Erran sat and put his hand on her arm. "Tell me," he said. "Tell me everything."

When she had gotten halfway through the story, Erran said, "Stop. I am going to take you before the council. Your story needs to be heard by more than just me."

An hour later four strapping members of the Ghee, the revered guards of the Batu people, were bearing her on a makeshift stretcher into the huge pyramid that housed the council. She was taken to the front of the council, through an utterly silent room, the eye of every councillor pinned to her.

When she reached the front of the chamber, she was seated on a gold chair reserved for honored speakers. To her horror she saw that both King Khalek and Prince Pelle were seated on a dias at the front of the room. To their left, Osa sat with the other councillors. Loor felt sick with self-disgust. She had been given a huge assignment. And she'd failed. Why were Erran and her mother putting Loor through this grotesque public humiliation? She'd have rather been taken out somewhere and flogged. But she had been trained never to show weakness. So despite her fatigue, her aching head, she kept her back straight, her chin high, her gaze imperious.

Out of the corner of her eye, she saw King Khalek nod to the chief councillor.

"My friends," Erran said, coming to the front of the chamber and standing next to her. "We entrusted this young warrior, barely more than a girl, on a mission of grave importance to our people just a little more than a week ago." Then he turned to her. "Loor, please give His Majesty your report."

Loor pushed herself to her feet. For a moment she thought she might faint. She tried to avoid her mother's eyes. But she couldn't. She expected her mother to look at her with contempt after hearing about Loor's failure. But instead, Osa's gaze was calm and reassuring. Loor shook off the urge to collapse.

Then she took a deep breath and began. Slowly at first, then gaining strength as she spoke, she told her story. She made no attempt to glorify her own actions or to excuse her failure. She simply told what happened.

When she was finished, there was a moment of silence. "I cannot apologize for my miserable performance," she said. "But I invite your harshest punishment for my failure. I do know where the ax is, however. I could not even hope to be entrusted with leading an expedition to find it after my failure here. But if I could just accompany—"

Erran cut her off with a sharp wave of his hand. "Silence."

She stopped speaking. She wanted to bow her head in shame. But she couldn't. She fixed her eyes on the very back of the chamber and clamped her jaw shut.

"Loor," Erran said. "I have misled you. Your true mission was not to find the ax. Axes can be made again."

Loor blinked. She looked from Erran to Osa. Osa looked away, a rare action for her.

"For years we Batu have needed to secure independent information about the sources of our water. Our dear friends, the Rokador, of course give us regular reports. But they do not allow us to inspect their works. We have sent many warriors into the desert to search the mountains for water." He paused portentously. "None have returned."

Loor swallowed. None of this made any sense at all.

"Finally we realized that without the support of the tribesmen, such a mission was impossible. And yet, never have we been able to secure their aid. So what were we to do?"

Heads nodded throughout the room. Loor remained frozen like a statue.

"Recently we had a stroke of good luck. The Ghee captured a raider from the desert, who told us that the ax would be stolen during the first day of Azhra. He told us—as you have explained—that the real goal of the theft was to draw an extraordinary woman from Xhaxhu so that she could be captured and taken by Zafir tribesmen as a bride for the king of their people. It was the unanimous opinion of everyone in this room that you were the right choice to be sent out."

"We didn't tell you because, had you known, you might have somehow given away your mission. If you had, the tribesmen would have killed you as a spy on the spot. So we deceived you."

Loor's head was spinning. She wanted more than anything else to sit down. But she remained rigidly at attention.

"Fellow councillors," Erran said, "Loor has succeeded in her mission beyond even what we had hoped. Despite the self-incriminating tone of her astonishing report, it is clear that she has demonstrated every single one of the highest virtues of the Batu people: strength, courage, self-discipline, humility, fighting spirit, military skill, stamina. . . ." He shook his head as though in amazement. "Because of her fortitude and determination, I move that this council award her Order of Supreme Merit and promote her forthwith to the rank of second level in the Ghee."

Loor could not believe it. She had been convinced that

she was on the verge of being severely and appropriately punished.

"If this girl has any flaw, it is that she—like most girls her age—retains a certain impulsiveness and rashness that time will surely temper." He then turned and bowed toward the old king. Loor followed suit.

King Khalek rose slowly from his chair. As he did, Crown Prince Pelle handed him a gold armband. The king then placed it around Loor's biceps. He was not a young man, but his grip was still strong.

As the king placed the symbol of the Order of Supreme Merit around her arm, the council rose in a body and applauded thunderously. The applause went on and on for minutes. Loor stared impassively at the floor, not even moving to wipe away the hot streams of moisture that ran from her eyes. When she looked up finally, she noticed that a tear was running down Osa's face too. Loor was amazed. She had never seen her mother cry, not once.

"Never make the first move," Erran whispered to Loor. "Never make the first move." Then he led her to the chair and sat her down.

Loor blinked, confused to hear the same words from Erran that had so recently come from the man she had fought in the desert.

The applause ended. There was a long silence in the chamber.

Then one of the councillors at the rear of the chamber rose and said, "How large would you say the so-called Lake of Peace was, Loor?"

Loor shook her head. "I could not say exactly. But it might have been as broad as the entire city of Xhaxhu."

There were shocked intakes of breath.

"You stated that the water does not flow out of the lake in a river."

"Yes," Loor said.

"Did it occur to you that perhaps it drains into the Rokador's underground river that you found running beneath the sand?"

Loor shrugged. "I—I do not know that I am competent to answer that question."

"Well, the water must go somewhere!" the councillor shouted.

"My friends, please," Erran said, "this poor girl is in a weakened state. We have prevailed on her enough. More details will reveal themselves eventually."

"This cannot wait!" shouted another councillor. "The Rokador are piping that water under the desert, and hiding it in some huge underground lake, while they let Xhaxhu wither up and die."

"Yes!" shouted another councillor.

"Now hold on!" a representative of the Rokador shouted, leaping to his feet. "I resent your accusations. For generations our people have sacrificed everything to bring—"

Erran lifted his hands again. "Please, brothers and sisters. Our goal in sending this young woman was not to create discord between Rokador and Batu, but to aid our Rokador friends in finding additional water sources."

"Do not be naive!" shouted a Batu counsillor. "Every time we bring up the subject of water, the Rokador give us this same speech about all of their terrible sacrifices and hard work, when in fact they are sitting around in their comfortable, cool underground palaces, while their hands are wrapped firmly around our throats. If we—"

For the first time King Khalek spoke. "Quiet!" he shouted. His voice was as strong and commanding as a parade-ground instructor. "There will be no more of this talk!"

Erran sighed. "I'm sorry, my dear," he whispered to Loor. "I did not want you to hear this. I will have the Ghee take you back to your hospital bed."

"I do not want to go back there—"

"Nonsense! Look at you. You are about to collapse. You have earned a rest," said Erran. He turned to the king.

King Khalek made a slight motion with his hand. Four Ghee jumped up and raised Loor on their shoulders. Within seconds she was being trundled away.

TEN

After she'd been taken back to the hospital, Loor had an argument with the nurse, tried to get up, and then collapsed back into the bed. As she was lying there, breathing heavily and fuming at her own weakness, the door opened and Erran entered.

The tall, distinguished councillor looked down at her. "The nurse tells me you have given her trouble," he said with a grin.

Loor frowned.

"Do you have anything you want to say?" Erran asked.

Loor shrugged.

"I am sure you are angry," he said. "We sent you into the desert under false pretenses."

Loor was feeling blindsided and confused by the whole situation. "I just tried to accomplish my mission. I still feel like I failed."

"What did you learn from the mission?" Erran said.

Loor thought of the instruction that both Erran himself and the one-eyed warrior had given her.

"Never make the first move," she said.

"Meaning what?"

She frowned. "I am too quick to attack. I entered that canyon full of those rock piles without checking to see what they were. If I had not been in such a hurry to attack, I would have realized that it was an ambush."

"So why does it serve you not to make the first move?"

"If you let the other person attack, they expose themselves. They reveal their strategy."

Erran studied her for a long time. She noticed for the first time that there was something odd about his eyes. All Batu had dark eyes. But Erran's eyes seemed to have a flickering blue depth to them.

"Good," he said finally. Then he stood, walked to the window, and looked out. "The thing one has to be aware of, of course, is that one's enemy may not show his hand on the first attack. What if the first blow is a ruse designed to reveal a false strategy? Maybe the real strategy lies below that. Or maybe one ruse is concealed beneath another."

Loor felt frustrated. This was too subtle for her. She interrupted him impatiently. "Then . . . how can you ever know?"

Erran turned and leaned against the window frame. "Well, that is the real problem. With the best strategy, no one *ever* really knows. Not until it's too late."

Loor sighed and leaned back in the bed. "This is making my head hurt," she said.

Erran laughed loudly. "Good," he said.

Loor didn't really see what was so funny. Erran was

an important man, and he seemed to have taken a lot of interest in her. Which was flattering. But she still wasn't quite sure what he was thinking.

"The important thing is that ultimately you made all the right decisions on your mission. That indicates good judgment. You can teach a person how to fight. You can teach a person how to add and subtract. You can teach a person to read. But you can't teach good judgment."

"I wonder . . . ," she said.

"What?"

"Well . . . every time I had a choice to make . . . the truth is, I just followed that silly bird."

Erran's eyes widened slightly. Not as if he were shocked. More like he was interested.

"I followed the hindor," she said. "That's all I did."

Erran raised one eyebrow, then shrugged lightly. "It brought you home, yes?" He smiled.

She rubbed her face. She felt like something was going on here, something underneath the surface. But she just couldn't figure it out.

"Yes . . . but . . . something has been bothering me," she said finally. Normally Loor felt certain about things. But right now she didn't. Maybe it was just because she was so weak. Or maybe it was something else. "I feel like everything that I found out is creating problems between us and the Rokador. Maybe we were better off not knowing how much water they have."

"Information is truth," Erran said firmly. "You led us to the truth."

"But are you sure that—"

Erran looked serious now. "I would never intentionally

create discord between our people and the Rokador," he said. "You must believe that."

"Well, of course!" she said. "I would never even *think* a thing like that."

"The Batu and the Rokador are like a brother and a sister." He splayed his fingers out, then intertwined them. "Family. You see? We need each other. Family."

After Erran was gone, though, she wondered. Erran had said that with the best strategy no one *ever* knows what you're up to. Erran had deceived her once. What if underneath all his talk of Batu-and-Rokador-as-family, he had some other plan?

Loor couldn't stop feeling that somehow she was being used. But how? She really couldn't be sure. What possible good could come out of conflict between the Rokador and the Batu?

As she was lying in her bed, staring at the ceiling, a man dressed in a doctor's garb appeared in the doorway. Strangely, he was not a dark-skinned Batu, but a pale-skinned Rokador. And yet there was something unusual looking about him. He was much darker than the normal pasty-faced Rokador. Dark like a desert tribesman, his skin tanned by the sun.

The odd-looking doctor glanced up and down the hallway, as though trying to make sure no one was watching him.

Loor sat up, alarmed. What if he were some desert tribesman sent here to kill her? What if . . . She let her fingers slide up to the knife that she kept hidden under her pillow.

But as soon as the stranger entered the room, a woman followed behind him. It was Loor's mother. "I've brought a visitor, Loor," Osa said.

"Hello, Loor," the man said, taking a seat next to her. "I hear you've had quite a revelatory week."

That was an odd way of describing almost dying in the middle of a desert. Loor nodded. "Maybe," she said.

"Well, buckle yourself in, kid," the odd-looking Rokador man said. "Things are about to get even stranger."

Buckle yourself in? What did that even mean?

Osa must have seen the skeptical look in Loor's eyes. "Loor," Osa said in her soft, firm voice, "I'm going to leave you two together. But understand that as strange as everything he says will be, it is all true." She stood. "Now I will leave you together."

Loor watched her go. For some reason she wanted her mother to stay. "Listen," the man said, leaning toward her. "Listen carefully. . . ."

As the man spoke, a shadow fell on his shoulder. Loor looked behind him. Perched on the ledge outside her window was a massive black bird. The hindor.

From a distance the hindor had always looked noble and regal, soaring slowly on the breeze. But now that she had a chance to study it, hunched there on the ledge, there was something about it that she didn't like, something coiled and hidden and savage. Maybe it was the eyes. They were like Erran's, now that she thought about it. At first glance they looked dark brown. But when you looked closer, you saw that they had a flickering blue depth. Strange. For a moment she thought—

But of course that was ridiculous. A man cannot change into a bird!

Loor shivered.

"I apologize," she said. "What were you saying? Something about a traveler?"

Siry Remudi

ONE

Sea trash. Siry Remudi had always been interested in things that rolled in from the sea. Strange things. Unusual things. Things which hinted that outside the comfortable, small village where he lived lay a vast and very different world.

So when the wave boiled in and smashed on the beach, and the odd-shaped thing rolled once and came to rest on the sand, Siry walked toward it.

It was about the size of a man, but it was made of strange, raglike material. He was several hundred feet away, so it was a little hard to tell. Maybe an odd bundle of seaweed? A log covered with algae or kelp? He started walking rapidly toward it. There was something intriguing about it.

Then the next wave crashed and another odd-looking object washed in. And another. And another.

He'd gotten within a hundred feet of it or so when the first object moved. It sat up. *That's no log!* Siry thought. *That's a man!*

Which was when he realized that the rags were clothes. Which meant—

He turned and began to run.

"Flighters!" he screamed. "Flighters! It's a raid!"

The Flighters were cut to pieces. There had been nine of them. They'd fought like demons. But they were no match—either in numbers or in skill—for the guards who'd come flocking out of the village of Rayne. One had drowned in the surf, two had fallen under the cudgels of the guards, five had escaped into the sea.

And one was captured.

After it was over, Siry caught a glimpse of the captive. He'd expected the Flighter to be a man. But it wasn't. It was a woman. Well, not even a woman. A girl.

She had struggled like an animal, scratching and shrieking as the guards dragged her off the beach and up toward the village. She had barely seemed human. Her clothes were wretched and falling apart. Her hair was matted. Her skin was streaked with dirt.

And yet there was something about her. As she was dragged off the beach, she passed within a few feet of Siry. Their eyes met briefly. She had brilliant green eyes, wide set, over a freckled, triangular face. Her hair was an astonishing red color unlike anything he'd ever seen before.

"Ahhhh!" she screamed, lunging at him. When Siry jerked backward in surprise, she spit on the ground and laughed at him.

The guards yanked her off her feet. "We'll see how funny you think that is after a couple of days in the hole!" one of them shouted. The girl kicked and wriggled, still laughing in a high, wild voice.

As they hauled her around the corner of a small hut, Siry's father, Jen Remudi, came around the corner. He had a gash on his arm and carried a club.

"There you are!" Siry's father said. "I was worried. I didn't see you anywhere."

"I'm fine," Siry said. He pointed in the direction that the girl had disappeared. "What are they doing with the prisoner?"

Jen sighed. "We'll have to put her on trial."

"For what?"

Jen frowned. "I forgot, you were barely five or six when the last wave of Flighter attacks happened. When we capture a prisoner, they're tried by the tribunal."

"And then what?"

Jen looked off toward the sea. "Best not to think of that, Son," he said.

Siry shrugged off his father's hand. "I'm not a kid anymore!" he said. He was tired of being treated as if he were five instead of fourteen. "Tell me what will happen to her."

Siry's father looked at him soberly. "I suppose you're right," he said. Then he sighed sadly. "They'll put her to death," he said finally.

"They?" Siry said. "Don't you mean *you*? You're a member of the tribunal."

Jen Remudi cocked his head. "What's gotten into you lately, Siry?"

Siry shrugged. He didn't know what his father was talking about.

Jen clapped his son on the shoulder and smiled. "Anyway, good work today. If you hadn't spotted those animals, there's no telling what might have happened. I'm really proud of you."

Siry looked out at the water. He wondered how they had gotten this far. Had they made a boat? It was common knowledge that Flighters were subhuman. A Flighter couldn't figure out how to make a boat. Maybe they'd stolen one.

He kept thinking of the strange girl. Only she could tell him the answer. He wanted to talk to her, find out what she knew. *Everything* she knew. Too bad Flighters couldn't talk.

"I gotta go, Dad," Siry said.

"Look, Siry," Jen said, "there's something I need to talk to you about."

"I gotta go," Siry said again.

Two

Siry kicked the sand as he wandered up the beach. Okay, so maybe his dad was right. He felt like he'd been in a bad mood all the time lately. And he couldn't quite put his finger on what it was that was bugging him.

It was just that it seemed as if—well, he remembered when he was younger, there had been times when adults had told him things that he knew weren't true. And when he confronted them, they'd always say things like, "Siry, you're too young to understand." As if he were supposed to be satisfied with that answer.

Back then it had just been little stuff. The time he'd figured out that all those presents that appeared overnight on Simmus Eve weren't really brought by fairies, for instance.

But now he was starting to feel it was bigger. Like all the sea trash he'd collected over the years—he was starting to be quite sure that some of it was man made. He'd found a piece of something, blue and flexible material that had raised letters on it. The letters didn't make any sense, but it was easy to see they were letters.

And yet when he showed it to his father, Jen had just said, "Well, I know it looks like letters. But it's probably just an accident. Some sort of coral maybe."

An accident? Did Jen really expect him to believe that?

Siry wandered off the beach and began shuffling through the town. Here and there, people called out to him. "Nice work, Siry!"

Siry didn't even acknowledge them. He just kept walking and thinking. No, there was something else out there. Something his dad wasn't telling him about. Something the elders were hiding. But what was it?

Without really making any particular decision, he found himself standing in front of the small hut where the occasional prisoner was held. Several guards stood outside. The hut was made from bamboo, topped with thatch. It hadn't been used much since most people in Rayne behaved themselves, so it was decrepit looking.

Siry knew both the guards pretty well. They were big, solid men, friends of his father.

"Hello, Kemo," Siry said. Kemo was the leader of Rayne's guards. "Is she in there?"

"Yes," Kemo said. He held up his arm, showing off a set of purple teeth marks on his skin. "Look at that, huh? You better believe I gave her a good hit after that, huh?" He grinned. "Nice job, spotting these animals."

Siry shrugged. "Hey, I was just standing there." He looked over Kemo's shoulder. There was a small window, barred with bamboo. "Can I look at her?"

Kemo narrowed her eyes. "Why such an interest in the Flighter?"

"I just want to look at her," Siry said.

Kemo waved at the barred window. "Just be careful. They're tricky. Don't get close or she's liable to try to attack you."

Siry walked over to the window and peered in. The Flighter girl was huddled on the floor. Her shoulder was bruised and there was a large cut on her leg.

"Hey," Siry said. "Can you talk?"

The girl didn't even look up at him. Siry studied her for a while. Other than being a little skinny, she looked perfectly healthy. If he'd seen her on the street, in different clothing, he'd never have known she was a Flighter.

As he was staring at her, a gaggle of little kids came by and joined him in the window, pointing and laughing at the Flighter. They were all eating juba nuts from a bag. After a minute one of the kids threw a juba nutshell at the girl. It bounced off her forehead and fell on the floor. Another kid threw a whole juba nut. It hit the girl in the face. The girl pounced on it, smashed it on the floor, and began picking the meat out of the broken nut.

Other kids began hurling nuts at the girl.

"Hey!" Siry said. "Stop!"

The kids backed away from him. One of them, a little girl with blond hair, started crying. Kemo gave Siry a nasty look. "Siry, what's wrong with you?" he said. "They're just kids having a little fun."

Siry turned back to the window. Inside, the girl began ravenously swallowing the nuts as if she'd never eaten before. When she was done, she went back to staring blankly at the floor.

After he'd stared at her for a while, he said, "Hey, Kemo. Who's bringing her food?"

Kemo's eyebrows went up. "Well—uh—usually when somebody's in the jail, their families bring them food."

"You're saying you don't have any food for her?"

Kemo shrugged. "I didn't really think about it."

"I'll go talk to my father," Siry said. "He'll have some food sent over."

Siry came back with a steaming bowl of vegetable and meat stew. Kemo let him into the front door. Inside was a small chamber in front of two separate cells. The girl was sitting in the exact same position she'd been in when he left. There was a slot near the floor that was obviously made for pushing food into the cell. Siry slid the bowl through.

"Sorry," Siry said to the girl, "I know it's nothing special. My mother died when I was young and my father only knows how to make two things. Vegetable and meat stew . . . and meat and vegetable stew." He laughed tentatively.

The girl showed no sign of hearing him, much less of thinking he was funny. She just grabbed the bowl and gobbled up all the stew, scooping it with her hands. He had given her a bamboo spoon, but she ignored it.

When she was finished, the girl threw the empty bowl at him and growled. The bowl clattered off the bamboo bars, splattering him with the remains of the stew.

Siry laughed. "Well, you have some bite, anyway," he said. He pushed a bucket of hot water and soap through the same slot as the food. "I don't know if you Flighters understand the concept of washing," he said. "But just in case . . ."

He made a motion with his hands, running them over his body as if he were bathing. The girl started drinking the water. Then she took a bite out of the soap, spit it on the ground. Siry laughed again.

The girl glared at him as if he'd tried to trick her.

"No. Soap," he said. "Soap!"

He reached through the bars, grabbed the soap off the floor. The girl made an attempt to stomp his hand, but he was too quick for her. "Nice try," he said with a grin. Then he rubbed the soap on his hands. "See? Clean. Like this." There was a large sink and a shower on the far side of the room. He demonstrated how soap worked. "Look. See? Nice and clean."

The girl stared uncomprehendingly at him. He tossed the bar of soap into the water. Then he pushed a set of clean clothes through the bars. "They were my mother's," he said. "I don't know if they'll fit. My father would be upset if he knew I was giving these to you. My mother's been dead for years. But he's never thrown out any of her things." He sat down on the chair opposite her cell. "It's kind of sad, you know? He still talks about her all the time. I guess he loved her a lot."

The girl took a piece of juba nutshell and started picking a piece of meat out of her teeth.

"She wasn't really my mother, though. I was adopted. My dad always says he found me floating on the waves. Isn't that a strange thing to say to your kid? I suppose it was a nice story when I was young. But now? It seems like an insult to my intelligence."

The girl finally freed the piece of meat from her teeth, held it out on the juba nutshell, looked at it, then popped it back in her mouth and swallowed.

"I have to say," Siry said, "your table manners could be better."

She spit on the floor.

After he left, Kemo put one large hand on Siry's arm. "Son, look, you probably don't remember the last time that Rayne had serious problems with the Flighters. We spent three solid years clearing the jungles and pushing those monsters back from Rayne."

"Okay . . . ," Siry said.

"What I'm saying is . . ." Kemo cleared his throat. "That thing in there—it looks as if you cleaned it up, it could be one of us. Don't be fooled. It can't be. It's an animal. It's sea trash. It's dangerous."

"Yes, sir," Siry said.

Kemo narrowed his eyes. "I'm serious, Siry. That thing in there'll kill you and rip your throat out. And it won't blink an eye."

"Yes, sir," Siry said.

But as he walked away, he felt sure that Kemo was wrong. The only question in his mind was this: Was Kemo lying? Or did he just not know better?

Later that evening, after they'd eaten supper together, he said to his father, "Where do Flighters come from?"

Jen Remudi broke his gaze from his son's. "The other end of the island," he said, staring down at the table.

The explanation didn't sit right with Siry. Somehow it seemed that these people were from somewhere farther, somewhere that would explain why they had become so different. "But—they look exactly like us. A little dirtier, but otherwise—"

"Appearances can be deceiving. They're not like us."

"But how would we know? We never talk to them. We never see them. All we do is fight them."

Siry's father looked back up at him, folding his hands together. "Look, Son, Kemo told me that you were talking to the girl we captured." He paused. "I know if you cleaned her up, she looks like she'd be pretty and sweet. But—"

"What are you *talking* about, Dad?" Siry said angrily.

"They don't feel things like we do."

"Feeling? Who's talking about feeling?" Siry said. "Every day I see stuff around here that doesn't seem to add up. Sea trash. What is it? Those bottle-shaped things with writing on them? Those pieces of flexible material that you can see through?"

"Don't fall in love with a Flighter. Okay?"

Siry stared at his dad. "I'm talking about trying to understand the world. And you're—I don't even know *what* you're talking about!"

There was a long silence. Finally his father said, "Son, she's going on trial the day after tomorrow. If the tribunal finds that she's broken our laws, she'll be . . ." He sighed. "She'll be put to death."

"Put to death!" Siry felt a strange lump in his stomach.

"It sounds cruel, I know. But you don't remember what it was like." He took a deep breath. "I've always told you that your mother died of a disease. But it's not so. Those things, those Flighters, they raided Rayne for food one time. There must have been close to a hundred of them. Breaking in to houses. Smashing things. Dragging children into the jungle. Your mother tried to stop them from taking you. They—"

Jen Remudi's eyes teared up.

Siry blinked. He felt horrible. But at the same time, he couldn't help thinking, *Another story that turns out not to be true!*

"She saved your life. But she gave up hers in the process." Jen Remudi put his face in his hands. Tears started running out through his fingers. "I couldn't save her. I should have been at the house. But I was with the guards, trying to protect—" He looked up, his eyes rimmed with red. "I love you so much, Son. But I just wish you had known her. I feel like I could have done so much better if—"

Jen stopped and stared out the window. "Anyway. The trial's in two days."

They sat in silence for a long time. Finally Siry stood up and said, "If they're animals, how come you give them a trial?"

Siry waited for his father to answer. But his father said nothing.

THREE

The next morning Siry brought three boiled eggs and some fruit to the Flighter girl.

Kemo was standing at his usual post. "Hey, Siry!" Kemo said. "I can't believe it."

"You can't believe what?"

"That animal. She actually used the soap you brought her. Put on those clothes, too. Amazing. You'd almost think she was human."

"Maybe she is," Siry said.

He went inside and pushed the food through the bars. Then he looked up. His eyes widened. The girl was wearing the clothes. And now that she was cleaned up? She was actually really pretty!

The girl ignored him. She just picked up the food and shoveled it in her mouth, dribbling bits of egg all over the floor.

"Still working on those manners, though?" he said.

She finished the food, then flopped down on the little cot in the corner, apparently ignoring him.

"What's it like out there?" he said. "I wish you

could tell me." He sat down in the chair on the other side of the bars from her. "You can't imagine how quiet it is here in Rayne. I just can't help feeling that there's more to life than *this*." He spread his hands. "Nice little town. Nice people. Nice school. Nice food. Nice weather. Everything's nice. But there's got to be something more. I bet you could tell me a lot. I mean, if you could just talk."

The girl belched.

Siry started babbling, talking about all the things that had been going through his head lately. All the questions he had about the world. All the fears and anxieties he had. All the feelings that he'd been keeping bottled up, that he'd tried telling his friends about. But no one had understood. All his friends had stared at him as if he were crazy when he started talking about sea trash, and where it came from.

"Sea trash," he said. "It just keeps coming back to sea trash. What is it? Where does it come from?" He took out a bag and spread it on the floor, showing her the bits of rusted metal, the hard clear material, the unnaturally flat and regular pieces of wood—and his biggest treasure, the flexible blue fragment with the writing on it.

Finally he put all his treasures back in the bag.

"I guess I must not make any sense to you," he said. "I talk and talk, and you have no idea what I'm saying."

He put the bag back on his belt.

"They're going to put you on trial tomorrow," he said. "And when they do? They'll execute you."

The girl sat up and walked toward him, her green eyes pinned on him. She grabbed the bars, her fingers almost touching his. Yesterday she had smelled horrible. Now she smelled soapy and clean.

"I'm sorry," he said, "but they're going to kill you."

Suddenly she reached though the bars and grabbed his arm. For a moment he was sure she was about to bite him or scratch him or stick her fingers in his eyes.

But instead she leaned close to him.

Then she spoke—a hoarse, uncertain whisper.

"Help. Me."

FOUR

Siry blinked, then flushed. If she could talk, then had she understood everything he'd said? All his complaining about Rayne must have seemed so childish. His life was far easier than life was for the Flighters, starving away off in the jungles on the far side of the island, or wherever they came from.

"You can *talk*?" he said.

She glared at him.

"But—everybody says—"

She looked out the window. "Help me." It seemed as though the words didn't come easily.

"Well . . . what do you want?"

"Do not." She looked at the floor. "Do not let them kill me."

"The tribunal."

She shrugged, pointed at the guards.

"Do you understand what's happening here?" he said. "You'll be tried in front of the tribunal. It's a group of important—look, if they find you guilty, they'll execute you."

She grabbed his collar and pulled him close to the bars. Her eyes were only inches from his. "Rena!" she hissed.

"Huh?"

"Rena." She tapped her own chest. "Me. Rena."

"Oh!" he said. "That's your name."

She nodded. "Me. Save."

Their faces were only inches apart. At first he'd been interested in her because she represented something to him—everything that was . . . *out there*. Everything that was not Rayne. But now? Now she seemed different. She wasn't just an idea. She was a person. Maybe not like everybody in Rayne. But still.

"I'll try," he said.

She let go of his collar.

Siry found his father at the building where the tribunal met. "So this trial . . . ," Siry said. "When does it happen?"

"First thing tomorrow morning," Jen Remudi said.

"What do you think is going to happen?" Siry asked.

"We'll present the facts. If the facts indicate that she was a raider who came here to break our laws and do us harm—" Siry's father shrugged.

"Who's going to defend her?"

"We'll pick a former member of the tribunal."

"Annik Neelow? She *hates* Flighters."

"We haven't decided. There are several other people who used to be on the tribunal."

"Yeah, and most of them are so old they can barely—"

"Look," his father interrupted, "we have a process. That's what separates us from the Flighters. It may not be perfect, but it's what we have."

Siry came to a decision on the spot. "I want to represent her."

Jen Remudi looked at his son for a long time. "Son, you're fourteen. You have no experience before the tribunal."

"Yeah, but I actually care if she lives or dies!" Siry said. It came out sounding a little more emotional than he wanted it to.

"Ah . . . ," Jen said, his eyes softening. He stroked his jaw thoughtfully. "Look, I don't really know how to say this. But you can't get your hopes up. You can't get involved with this girl."

"Involved?" Siry said angrily. "What's that supposed to mean?"

"I'm just saying—"

"There's more to her than meets the eye."

"You're always saying that, Siry," his father said. "I'm not saying you're always wrong. But you're not always right, either. Sometimes things are *exactly* what they seem to be."

Siry fixed his eyes on his father, challenging him. "And sometimes they're not."

Jen Remudi looked away. "I'll think about it," he said finally. "You're a smart kid. And I know you'll do everything you can. But I'm not making any promises."

After his conversation with his father, Siry went to the beach. Several of his friends—Loque, Twig, and some others—were already there, swimming in the surf.

"Hey!" Twig called. "Heard you've been over to see that girl we captured."

Nellah, a blond girl about a year older than Siry, said, "They're gonna execute her, you know. I don't see why you're wasting your time."

"We'll see," Siry said.

Nellah's eyes narrowed. "Those animals were here to kill us!" she shouted. "Last week May Lonati was gathering fruit outside the village. One of them hit her with a rock and stole all her fruit. If a guard hadn't happened to show up, the Flighters would have killed her."

"You don't know that."

"Come on! Don't be stupid." She turned and looked at Siry's friends. "I mean we all know what's going on here, don't we?"

Everyone nodded.

"Siry," said Loque, "I know you mean well. But Flighters are not like us. They'd destroy our whole way of life just like that." He snapped his fingers. "And they wouldn't even care."

Siry's jaw worked. "So you don't even think we should defend them in front of the tribunal."

Loque looked thoughtful.

Before he could speak, though, one of the other kids said, "Let's be serious. The tribunal is a formality. We all know what has to be done here."

Siry looked around the circle. "You're saying if I go in there and defend her, no matter what I say . . ."

Everyone looked at him without speaking.

Finally Twig shrugged. "Forget her, Siry." She kicked

something that had just rolled in on a wave, a flash of something white in the sand. The white thing flew through the air and disappeared into the boiling surf. "Sea trash. It rolls in, it rolls out. You can't be thinking about it all the time."

Siry shook his head. "This isn't right."

Everybody looked at him for a minute. Then Twig splashed Nellah, and Nellah splashed Loque, and the next thing Siry knew, all of the kids were swimming around and laughing.

Siry watched them silently. Sometimes he got the feeling that this group could be more than just a bunch of kids goofing around. There was something they could do—together—that would be important and meaningful. But he just couldn't get a handle on what it was.

He started to make an argument about why the Flighter girl should be saved. But as he watched his friends splashing aimlessly in the water, he knew it was pointless. Now wasn't the right time for . . . whatever it was that was building in his mind.

As he thought about what he could do to save the Flighter girl, it struck him that these were his friends, people who actually listened to him (most of the time anyway!). If his friends were this quick to ignore him and to write off the girl, then he could just imagine what everybody else in Rayne would be like.

When Siry got home that night, his father stood in the front door, his face tight with anger.

"Did you do it?" he said. He didn't raise his voice. Which was always a bad sign.

"Do what?"

"You know exactly what I'm talking about." Jen Remudi had a piece of bright-colored cloth in his hand, which he shook in Siry's face.

"I don't!"

"I found this on the floor next to the box where your mother's clothes are stored."

Siry said nothing.

"You gave your mother's clothes to that . . . that . . . that . . ." He couldn't seem to find a word bad enough to call the Flighter girl.

"Rena," Siry said. "Her name is Rena."

"Her people *killed* your mother!" Jen said. "I'm ashamed of you."

Siry faced his father. "Rena was a child when that happened. It's not her fault!"

His father was literally trembling with anger. "I can't even talk to you," he said. "I'm afraid of what I might say."

He stomped off into the house.

"Can I represent her tomorrow?" Siry shouted after him.

His father turned and looked at him. "Do whatever you want. Obviously, you won't listen to reason."

"Reason? What do you think this is all about? It's *all* about reason!" He was going to add that he was tired of fairy stories and half-truths.

But his father walked away before he could finish saying all the words that felt as if they were ready to burst from his chest.

"The truth can't hide forever!" Siry shouted. He

noticed that now he was trembling with anger too. He wasn't even sure what he was talking about though. Was he talking about the Flighter girl? Or something else?

That night Siry lay in his bed staring at the thatch ceiling of his room. For a long time he practiced what he was going to say. She was only a girl. She had a name. Look at her. She was clean. She could speak. How was she any different from any other kid in Rayne? He had a lot of arguments to make. He practiced simple phrases, fancy flights of rhetoric, sharp questions, hard-nosed demands. . . . But no matter how he phrased things in his head, he kept coming back to the expression on his father's face.

They hated her. They all did. What were they so scared of?

FIVE

Almost the entire population of Rayne were present. Seated in the front of the space, behind a large table, were the members of the tribunal. Each of them wore a light green uniform with long sleeves and long pants. Their faces were all stern and expressionless. Siry tried not to look too long at Jen Remudi sitting among them.

Rena was ushered toward the front by two large guards. As she walked forward, people in the crowd shouted at her. Her hands were bound behind her. She muttered to herself and occasionally tried halfheartedly to free her hands. But she seemed oblivious to the crowd.

Finally she stopped and was forced to sit. She snarled at the guards, shook herself like a dog, then was still.

The head of the tribunal stood. "As chief minister I hereby convene this tribunal," he said. "The purpose of this proceeding is to determine whether the accused has violated the laws of the village of Rayne. If, upon the determination of the tribunal, she has violated our laws, she will be punished in accordance with those laws. Lema, please rise and deliver the charges."

A slim, middle-aged woman stood and read from a sheet of paper. "The accused, Rena No-Last-Name, has been accused with the following violations of law: Raiding. Theft. Aggravated assault. Attempted murder. Trespass. Resisting arrest. Escape . . ." She droned on for a while, reading off a litany of charges.

Siry felt his stomach turn. His father had agreed to let him speak for Rena. But he wouldn't have his chance until after Lema delivered her evidence.

After reading the charges, Lema called a variety of witnesses to the stand, including Kemo and several other guards. There were no surprises in the testimony. They simply described how the handful of Flighters had emerged from the sea, run up into the village, turned over a cart full of fruit, and then fought everyone who got close to them. Rena herself had knocked one guard unconscious with a stick, and scratched another across the face so deeply that he had to be stitched up.

Each time a witness concluded his testimony, the chief minister turned to Siry and said, "Do you have questions for the witness?"

Each time Siry replied, "No."

All told, the testimony took about an hour.

When they were done, the chief minister said, "Siry, you have been appointed to represent the accused. Do you have any witnesses?"

Siry stood up. His legs felt like water and his hands were shaking. He pointed. "I call—" His voice cracked. A couple of girls in the crowd giggled. He cleared his throat. "I call the Flighter girl to the stand." He pointed to the witness chair.

There were snickers from the crowd. They obviously thought the idea of a dumb brute testifying was absurd.

"Would you, uh, go sit there please."

After a moment the Flighter girl shuffled up to the seat, flopped down sullenly, and stared up at the sky.

Siry took a deep breath. His heart was beating wildly. Every single person in the village was staring at him. He willed himself to calm down.

"Could you please say your name," Siry said.

More laughter from the crowd.

"Your name. Please tell me your name."

Their laughter died out. Rena surveyed the crowd, her eyes narrowed. Finally she said, "Rena. My name . . . Rena."

Someone gasped. The crowd stirred. This was unexpected. Apparently no one had ever heard a Flighter talk. After a moment the noise died down.

"Where do you come from, Rena?"

She pointed at the forest. "There."

"You are being charged with a crime under the laws of Rayne. Do you understand that?"

Rena looked at him but didn't answer.

"Rena, please answer."

"Why?" she said.

"Rena. I explained what laws are, right?"

"Laws nothing. Just talk. You want kill Rena? Nothing stop." She looked at the crowd, then thumped her chest. "Do it. Kill Rena."

The crowd murmured. "Good idea!" shouted someone. This provoked a great deal of laughter.

Siry looked furiously at the head of the tribunal. "Make them stop!"

The chief minister scowled, then thumped the table with his gavel. "We'll have quiet!"

Siry turned back to Rena.

"Rena, why did you come here?"

She looked at him as though he were stupid. "Hungry." She made a circle over her head with one finger. "Here, food."

"Rena, how old are you?"

Rena shrugged.

"Do you know what a year is? Do you understand numbers?"

Rena said nothing.

"How many summers have you lived through? Five?" He held up five fingers.

Rena rolled her eyes.

"Ten?" He held up both hands, fingers extended.

Rena looked at him for a moment, then shook her head.

"Fifteen?" he said

She held up ten fingers, then four. "This many."

There was a mutter from the crowd.

"Thank you. You can sit down."

Jen Remudi said, "That's it, Siry?"

"Yes," Siry said.

Lema rose and said, "If I may, let me summarize the charges and the evidence propounded for each charge, such that—"

Siry raised his hand and interrupted. "Uh, is this necessary?"

"Of course it's necessary," his father said.

"Well, what I mean is this," Siry said. "It's all true."

The crowd stirred and muttered.

Rena's head whipped around. "Lie!" she shouted. "You lie! You say you help!"

"Wait, wait!" Siry held up his hands. "If you'll bear with me—"

"Lie! Lie! Lie!"

"Have her restrained and gagged!" the chief minister shouted. He waited as the guards grabbed the struggling girl and shoved a piece of cloth into her mouth.

When she finally stopped wrestling with the guards, Siry said. "No one can say the facts here aren't true. She and her friends swam here through rough surf, came up the beach, and knocked over a table. According to the testimony, they managed to steal one mango." He held up his index finger. "One."

The crowd stirred restlessly.

"Rena and her friends were immediately surrounded by a bunch of hostile guards. Who attacked whom? Hard to say. What it comes down to is, they started fighting. In the course of the fight, Rena and her friends beat up a couple of guys. In return, three of them were killed, five were driven into the ocean, and then we put Rena in prison, to be executed."

The crowd was silent. No one moved. A soft wind rustled the trees.

Siry walked across the entire open area. He was starting to feel more confident now. He could feel the crowd hanging on his every word. This was actually kind of exciting, now that he'd captured everyone's attention.

On the table where he'd been sitting was a beautiful ripe mango. He picked it up, held it in one hand, high in the air. Then he walked back in the direction he'd come, displaying the mango to the crowd.

"One mango. A fourteen-year-old girl treks through the jungle, swims through a riptide, and undergoes the risk of violent death at the hands of trained fighters like my friend Kemo, just to get one of these."

The crowd was uncomfortably silent.

He shrugged. "Hey, I know what they say about Flighters. They're not like us. Brutes. Animals. Monsters." He pointed at Rena. "Does she really look like a monster to you? She even talks a little." He paused. "I don't know. I think maybe those Flighters over there are kind of like us."

The crowd stirred.

"They're like us . . . except they don't have tools, or decent fields for growing food, or boats, or whatever is up there in that mountain that makes the lights work in our houses." He pointed up at the mountain looming over the village. "I mean we've got all the good land over here. Anybody who's ever been to the other side of the island knows it's a rocky jungle with bad soil. Rena's people have nothing."

The crowd was utterly and completely silent. The only sound was the wind. That and Rena's soft weeping. Siry walked over to her, pulled the gag out of her mouth. She was sobbing openly now.

"What do we know about these people?" He pointed at the sobbing girl. "Nothing. So how come we're so sure that we're better than they are?"

He pulled out his belt knife and cut the cords that held Rena's hands. He set the mango in front of Rena. She stared at it morosely.

He took a deep breath. He could feel something rising inside of him. A feeling of triumph. He had them now. "I would say, people of Rayne, that if anything makes us better, it's that we believe in justice, and compassion. We believe in forgiveness."

Heads were nodding throughout the crowd. Even his father, the hard-bitten Jen Remudi, nodded once.

Siry pointed at the girl. "She's fourteen years old. Fourteen! And we're actually standing here talking about killing her? For this?" He picked up the mango. "Maybe if what we're trying to do here is get justice, then we should take her in, feed her, give her clothes, treat her like one of us. Maybe she'll never learn to talk properly or think like we do. But maybe we can show her that there is another way."

Siry walked over, picked up the mango from in front of Rena, then set it on the table in front of his father. He walked over and sat down next to Rena.

The wind stirred the palm trees for a while. And then the people of Rayne began to applaud.

Six

The chief minister found a family who was willing to take Rena in. But she didn't seem to be settling in very well. She rarely spoke to anyone. In fact, she made no attempts to make friends. She couldn't read or write, and showed no interest in school. Siry was the only person she spent any time with. And that was more because of his efforts.

Siry tried to take her aside and teach her the alphabet, teach her more words, but she just sighed and rolled her eyes. He wasn't completely sure why he felt so drawn to her. She was sort of pretty. But he didn't think about her the way he thought about other girls. It was more as if she were a puzzle, like something he needed to figure out. But the more time he spent with her, the more frustrated he became.

"Look," he said finally one day after spending an hour unsuccessfully trying to teach her the alphabet. "If you're going to stay here, you're going to have to start trying to understand how we do things."

"Why?" she said. She held up the book he'd been trying to teach her to read. "Can't eat book."

"Come with me," Siry said.

He led her silently down the path from Rayne, up to the base of Tribunal Mountain, which loomed over the village. As they skirted the top of a small cliff above the sea, they reached a large steel door set into the face of rock.

"I can't tell you everything that's back there," he said. "Honestly, I don't even know. But I can tell you that the smartest people in Rayne all come up here every day and disappear into this mountain. They keep it locked up tight. I mean, let's face it, you don't lock up things that aren't valuable, do you?"

Rena stared blankly at the door into the mountain.

"They're not gathering fruit, Rena. They're not fishing. They're not doing anything like that. But those wires that come into our houses, the ones that make the light so we can see at night? It all comes out of here."

She shrugged. He had tried to explain about the way lights worked. But she had just pointed at the lights and said, "Magic." He tried to think of something that would make more sense to her. "Butter!" he said. "Cheese. All those good foods that you can't just shake off a tree? They all come from behind that door."

She cocked her head. But still she said nothing, asked no questions. As long as he could remember, Siry had been fascinated by the mountain. Things happened in there that nobody talked about. But the girl just didn't seem to understand.

"Maybe it's because you haven't been here as long as I have," he said. "Why do they not talk about what they do in there? Why do they pretend like it's nothing?"

A large tree stood next to the door, a wild grapevine twining up the trunk. Littered on the grass were hundreds of wild grapes. Many lay spoiling on the ground and a heavy, winy smell hung over the place. As the wind stirred the tree, a few grapes fell down onto the ground. Rena walked over, picked up a grape, sniffed it, popped it in her mouth. She chewed it with her eyes closed and smiled. "Mmmmm!" she said.

Siry pursued her. "You're really not interested?" he said. Sometimes he wasn't sure how much she actually understood of what he was saying.

"The door's locked. But I've been inside parts of it with my father. The tribunal meets in this huge room here. One time I saw a room that had thousands and thousands of books. I wasn't supposed to go in there, but I did. I looked in one of the books and it described machines. Amazing machines. I couldn't even figure out what they did. But they were like nothing I've ever seen here."

Rena sat on the ground and started picking up wild grapes and popping them in her mouth.

"Don't you have even a *shred* of curiosity?" he asked. "Why are we different from you Flighters? The answer's behind that door."

"No need answer. Already got."

"Yeah?" Siry smiled. "So tell me. What's the difference between you and us?"

Rena's expression was matter-of-fact. "Food," she said.

"Food?"

"Food," she said. "You got food. Lots."

"Yeah, but why? Because we grow crops, that's why. Because we raise animals that we can eat. Because we have tools that help us with the crops. Because we know how to fertilize the ground and—"

"Us? Flighters?" Rena slapped her chest. "All day. Look food. Look food. Look food. Always. Hungry. Always. Come far"—she swept her hand out toward the water—"find food."

Siry's eyebrows raised. *"Come far?"* So was it true, then, that the flighters came from somewhere farther than the other side of the island?

He wanted to keep her talking, to learn more. Suddenly it felt as if all the questions he'd always had were more relevant than ever, and the answers even closer. "Yes! Right! That's what I'm saying! There's a reason." He pointed at the door. "I don't know what's in there. But there's something. There's something that's hidden. There's something they're not telling us. Something that helps us make all the food we can possibly eat."

Rena's eyes were scanning the ground, looking for more grapes.

"Don't you want to know more? Don't you feel angry that things are being hidden from you?"

Rena hunched over, plucked grapes off the ground, stuffed them in her pockets. The grapes left purple stains on her clothing. But Rena clearly didn't care.

"Why do you think you're hungry all the time? Because of knowledge! We have knowledge! All the stuff that gives us here in Rayne better lives than you guys who live on the other side of the island."

"Food?" She pointed at the door in the side of the mountain.

Siry shook his head. "Yeah. Maybe. But that's not the point. What's in there is bigger than food."

Rena walked to the door, yanked on the handle. The steel door was locked and wouldn't budge. She kept yanking.

"Food," she said. "Food."

Siry sighed and shook his head.

"Food?" she said, grapes spilling out of her pockets.

"Yes!" Siry said, exasperated. He felt as if he were talking to a three-year-old. "Yes, I'm sure there's probably food in there! But there's all kinds of stuff, stuff that's a lot more interesting than food. Books. Machines. Tools."

She continued to stuff grapes in her pockets.

"There's also magic in there!" Siry said desperately. "Magic things that fly through the air and control the weather and change rocks into fish. Magic that you can use to create endless supplies of food."

Rena's eyes widened. Now she looked up from the grapes. "Magic?"

Siry sighed loudly. This was a total waste of time.

Rena's eyes took on a cunning look. She approached the door, touched it lightly with her fingertips. "Get in? How?"

"There's a key," Siry said. "It's stored in the administration building in the village."

Rena looked at the door for a while longer. Then she turned and started walking down the path back toward Rayne.

"There's no such thing as magic!" Siry shouted after

her. "There's only *knowledge*! Facts! Reason! Understanding!"

But Rena just kept walking, eating grapes out of her pockets.

The next day after school Siry found Rena sitting on the beach, staring out at the sea. He had brought his little bag of sea trash, thinking it might get her interested in reading.

He dumped a few of the items on the sand in front of her. "Look," he said, picking up half a bottle made from clear blue material. There were raised letters visible on the surface. "See: a-s-p-i-r-i-n. It's a word. I don't know what it means. But it means *something*. Someday I'll find out."

She shrugged.

"You can't live without dreams!" he said. "This can't be *it*!" He waved his arms around, taking in the little village, the little island, the strip of sand, the featureless horizon. "There's more. There's something bigger. Someday I'll find it. You'll see!"

She looked blankly at the little shard of clear material. After a minute she put it in her mouth. She chewed it for several seconds, then spit it out.

"Trash," she said.

"But what if some trash isn't really trash?" he said. "What if it seems like trash, but actually it's a message? Some kind of information or secret. Some kind of knowledge."

Rena looked out at the sea. Then she turned and pointed up at Tribunal Mountain. "Magic?" she said finally.

"Joke!" Siry said angrily. "There's no such thing as magic. That was a joke."

"Give us magic," she said. "Everybody happy. Make stones into fish."

Siry put his face in his hands.

SEVEN

She's gone."

"What?" Siry was just finishing his breakfast, a ripe mango, as his father walked into the house.

"She's gone," Jen Remudi repeated.

Siry was confused. "Who? Who's gone?"

"Your sweet little friend Rena. She took off in the middle of the night." It was rare that Jen Remudi carried a weapon. But today he was clutching a short, heavy club—the kind that was carried by Rayne's guards.

"She'll be back," Siry said morosely. "After all, we have food."

"That's what I'm afraid of," Jen said.

"What do you mean?"

"The key to the tunnels in the mountain. She took it with her."

Siry had a bad feeling, like he'd been standing on a very high platform . . . and it had just given way. "There must be some mistake. Maybe they misplaced it."

"The master key is kept in a locked box in the

tribunal administration house. The lock was smashed. The key is gone."

Siry swallowed.

"Siry, why would she do that?"

Siry took a deep breath. "Look, there's something in that mountain, isn't there? Nobody will admit it, but there's something in there."

"Siry, I asked you a question. Why would she have taken that key?"

"Tell me what's in there. I have a right to know!"

Jen Remudi's face hardened. "Son, you're fourteen years old. There are things you are not ready to know. Things you may *never* be ready to know."

Siry felt a flash of anger. "What do you mean?"

"Tell me why she took that key."

"No! Not till you tell me what's in the mountain."

Siry's father grabbed his hand. He was a large, strong, imposing man. "Do you think I'm here to *bargain* with you?" Jen Remudi shouted. "Why did she take the key?"

"Tell me what's in the mountain and I'll tell you why." Siry tried to snatch his hand away from his father's grip and get up out of his chair.

Jen Remudi slammed his son backward into the seat. Siry felt a burst of anger at his own powerlessness. He struggled and wriggled in his father's powerful grasp. Suddenly the chair gave way, and both Siry and Jen pitched over, slamming Siry's head on the floor.

For a moment everything went black. Then, as Siry recovered his senses, he saw his father standing over him.

"Look what you made me do!" Jen Remudi said. "Do you think I want to do this to you?"

Siry sat up slowly. There was a sharp pain in the back of his head.

"Why did she take the key?" Jen Remudi demanded.

Momentarily stunned, Siry didn't have the strength to resist him. He touched the back of his head. It felt wet.

"I told her there was magic inside the mountain," Siry said. "Magic that you could use to make food."

He took his hand away from his head. It was smeared with blood.

Jen Remudi sighed loudly, a look of pain crossing his face. He dropped his club on the ground and picked Siry up like a baby. "Why would you tell her a thing like that?" he said softly.

Siry shrugged. "I was just trying to get her interested in something."

Jen Remudi carried his son to the sink, washed off the back of his head with a cloth. It was an odd sensation lying there, cradled in his father's powerful arms. On one hand it was comforting. But on the other, it made him feel helpless. And when Siry felt helpless, he felt angry. He wasn't a little kid anymore.

Siry pushed his father's hand away. "I'm fine, Dad."

"Let me just—"

Siry slipped from his father's grasp. "I'm *fine!*" he said.

Jen Remudi put his hand on Siry's shoulder. "Son, look, you meant well. Everything you did, you did from your heart. You tried to help somebody. I'm proud of you for that."

Siry hated it when Jen said things like that. He shrugged off his father's hand, then stooped to the floor to pick up the mango he'd been eating. There was dirt on it now. He threw it angrily in the trash.

"Son," his father continued, "she doesn't think like we do. I'm not saying she had some big plan to take advantage of you. But that's what's happened. She took advantage of your generosity. And now she's going to use it against us. Against all of us."

"Why can't you just tell me what's in the mountain, Dad?" Siry shouted. "Why can't you people just be honest? Why do you have to lie? Why do you have to hide things?"

"All right, forget it." Jen Remudi threw the bloody washrag in the sink. "I try and I try and I try. And you just refuse to listen to anything I say."

"Lies!" Siry shouted. His head was throbbing. He felt halfway like crying and halfway like hurling himself at his father. "Lies, lies, lies!"

Jen Remudi stuck his finger in his son's face. "Son, you need to think really hard before you say another—"

Siry's father was interrupted by a shout. "Flighters!"

Siry and his father both looked up.

"Flighters!" came the shout again. "They're attacking!"

"Stay here!" Jen Remudi vaulted to his feet, grabbed the heavy club he'd been carrying.

"Flighters!" came another cry. "Help!"

The calls were coming from the edge of the jungle on the west side of Rayne. "Do not move!" Jen shouted. "If they come, hide in the cellar!"

Siry's father turned and tore off down the street. Siry watched him go with a strange mix of pride and anger as the big man charged down the street with his smooth athletic gait. It seemed like no matter what Siry did, he would always fall short of the mark his father set.

Siry thought about everything that his father had just said. Had Rena really stolen the key that would give away the secret of whatever was in the mountain? Maybe in some little part of his brain, he'd known all along that this was what would happen. Maybe he had actually hoped she'd break in there and reveal whatever secret was hiding inside.

But another part of him didn't believe she'd betray him. After all that he'd done for her? He'd saved her life! Could she have wandered off into the jungle and betrayed what he told her to the Flighters?

But the fact that the Flighters were here, just a matter of hours after she'd left? The conclusion was pretty hard to escape. His father was probably right. She'd used him. And now everybody in Rayne was going to pay for his stupidity.

Siry's face burned with shame.

"Flighters!" another voice yelled—closer this time. "Help! They're everywhere!"

Siry ran to a cupboard. But not to hide. His father had been teaching him the rudiments of club fighting. And, being perfectly modest, he was getting pretty good.

Siry grabbed the club he'd been training with and ran out of the house. He could hear the sound of a raging battle. Screaming, yelling, confusion—it was obvious from the sounds that this was a major attack.

He sprinted toward the noise. As he rounded the corner, he saw several of his friends standing in the middle of the road, looking wide eyed. "What are you standing there for?" he called. "Grab your clubs and follow me!"

The other kids looked at one another nervously.

Sensing that what his friends needed was firmness and leadership, Siry lifted his club and waved it in a circle. "Hurry!" Siry shouted. "We've got to help!"

His outburst shocked them into action. Within seconds he was at the head of a wedge of eight or nine boys and girls, all of them carrying clubs. As they sprinted over the small rise on the west side of Rayne, Siry saw an astonishing sight.

There must have been several dozen Flighters— dirty, ragged, hollow eyed. Individually they didn't look like much. But there were a lot of them. And more important, they had caught the people of Rayne flat footed. The villagers hadn't had time to form a decent defensive perimeter. A phalanx of guards was holding their own in the center. But flanking the guards were normal people—less well trained, less organized. They were falling back in panic.

People from the village were still arriving. But many of them hadn't had time to grab clubs. Some of them were armed with only kitchen knives or even just their bare hands.

The Flighters, on the other hand, clearly had a plan. Maybe not a complex plan. But a plan nevertheless. Their tallest, strongest-looking men were in the center. Siry saw the biggest of them, a dark towering giant, locked in furious combat with Kemo. Siry's father was among the fighters too, swinging coolly and methodically with his club as he called out encouragement and instructions to the guards.

Siry looked frantically to see if Rena was among the attacking Flighters. She wasn't. *Maybe the attack is a coincidence,* he thought hopefully. Maybe she hadn't betrayed him. Maybe she was wandering around in the woods somewhere, oblivious to all of this.

But he wasn't sure that he really believed it.

"Over there!" Siry shouted, pointing his club toward the far side of the line of attacking Flighters. "We have to turn them back before that flank gives way!"

He led his friends toward the far flank. As the young people arrived, the villagers were wavering under the onslaught of the Flighters.

"Hold the line! Hold the line!" Siry shouted encouragement to the frightened villagers on the flank. "You can do it!"

"Join the line," shouted Loque.

"No," Siry shouted back. "We'll outflank them and roll them back."

He didn't wait for assent; he just sprinted around the ragged line of combatants. His friends all followed his lead and charged, howling, into the ragged group of Flighters.

The Flighters were taken by surprise. Siry pounded one desperate-looking Flighter on the arm. The man screamed in pain, dropped his club and staggered backward. Siry engaged another man, tripped him, and hit him twice in the face. The man sagged to the ground unconscious. Within moments the left flank of the Flighters was in disarray.

Siry felt a burst of excitement. His plan was working! He had never quite seen himself as a leader. But now he realized that some of the same qualities his father had, flowed in his own veins.

"Woooooo!" shouted Twig.

"Yaaaaahh!" shouted Loque.

Fighting was a heady mix of complete panic and complete focus and concentration. Siry bared his teeth and hammered away at an opponent. The man's stick grazed his face. But he barely even felt it. Another stroke of his club broke the man's stick. His eyes widened and he dodged backward.

The momentum of the battle had began to shift. The sudden arrival of ten aggressive and fearless kids, attacking in coordinated fashion, had thrown the entire Flighter plan off. There were still more Flighters on the field than there were people from Rayne. And the guards were being driven slowly backward. But the flanks of the Rayne line were no longer looking quite so flimsy, and more villagers were arriving every minute.

Siry kept scanning, looking for Rena. He wanted to believe that these people weren't here because of her. But it just didn't stand up to logic. Maybe she hadn't come here with the specific goal of spying on the town. But that's how it had worked out. The two weeks she'd spent here had given her a chance to see every vital target and every weak point in the village. And now the Flighters were attacking based on the information she had brought back.

But where was she?

And that's when he realized what was going on. He turned to Twig. "This is just a diversion!" he shouted, dodging a rock thrown by a young Flighter woman. "We have to get to the mountain."

"But they need us here!" Twig shouted back. Despite the apparent shift in momentum, the fight was still raging.

"If we leave, they'll—"

Siry shoved a Flighter backward. "Look, there are more of our people coming all the time. They're going to be okay here. We need to get over to the mountain. Now!"

"The what?" Twig was dodging and weaving as a larger Flighter tried to hit her with a tree branch.

"The *mountain*."

Without another word Siry turned and started running toward the trail that led along the cliff and up to the mountain. His heart was pounding and adrenaline was still shooting through his veins.

Only four of Siry's friends had joined him. The others had apparently decided to stay.

"What are we doing?" shouted Loque as they ran up the path leading to the mountain.

"It's Rena!" he said. "She has the key to the mountain tunnels. I think she's leading a raid."

They pounded wordlessly up the trail, through a stand of palm trees and out onto the small clearing in front of the entrance to the tunnels that ran through the mountain. The clearing stood at the top of a small cliff that hung over the crashing surf.

In front of the door were two guards. And close to ten Flighters.

"Get 'em!" Siry shouted. He and his friends charged toward the knot of Flighters, shouting at the tops of their lungs.

As they charged, Siry spotted two green eyes surrounded by long red hair. Rena seemed to look right through him, almost as though she had never known him at all. He spotted the large iron key in her hand.

One of the guards was bleeding heavily from a nasty cut on his scalp, and the other was barely managing to keep the attacking Flighters away from the door. These Flighters, Siry noted, looked stronger and better fed than most of the ones in the larger battle over by the village. And other than Rena, they were all older and bigger than Siry and his friends.

Instinctively Siry knew that the only way to beat them would be to remain organized. "Shoulder to shoulder," he said. "Keep tight! There are more of them than of us. But if we keep a tight formation, they can't attack us two on one."

The five kids came to a halt near the door, lifted their clubs, and began marching forward. The knot of young Flighters turned to engage them.

"Get in front of him," Siry called, pointing at the wounded guard.

The wounded guard fell back with relief. It was obvious he didn't have much fight left in him. Siry and the others began striking at the larger group of Flighters. Though the Flighters were aggressive and angry, it was clear they had no training whatsoever. They flailed wildly. And their sticks were light, flimsy, made of poorly chosen wood.

"Thanks for the help!" the remaining guard shouted.

"It's not over yet," Siry said. "Don't let Rena get to the door."

And in fact, she was already edging forward, trying to use the Flighters in front of her as cover so she could reach the door.

"If they get inside, they can bar the door and then destroy everything!" Siry called. That was what was at stake, he realized. If the Flighters disabled or destroyed whatever was inside the mountain . . . Well, he felt sure it would just be a matter of time before Rayne was in nearly as bad shape as the Flighters. And then the more numerous Flighters would probably be able to overwhelm the village.

Several of the Flighters seemed to be hanging back, not all that interested in risking their lives. But the ones in front were committed. They flailed away with abandon. Siry spotted their leader immediately. He was the biggest Flighter, a tall blond young man with a scar running down the side of his face.

Right now the leader was still engaged with the remaining guard. Siry made up his mind to look for an opportunity to take him out.

But in the meantime one of the Flighters leaped forward. His stick came down with a sickening crack on Twig's shoulder. Twig screamed and fell to the ground clutching her arm.

But Siry managed to use the Flighter's leap to counterattack. By jumping away from his compatriots, the Flighter had exposed himself. Siry landed two swift blows to the Flighter's neck, and the Flighter fell to the ground, gasping horribly.

There was a brief break in the fighting. Siry saw that Rena had almost reached the door. "Stop her!" he shouted.

The guard leaped to his right, trying to stop Rena from reaching the entrance. As he did, though, he opened himself to attack from the scarred young Flighter, who swept the guard's feet out from under him, then hit him in the head. The guard went down like a puppet with its strings cut.

But Siry saw his moment. The fighters had moved closer to the cliff edge as they struggled. If he could time it right . . .

He charged forward, grabbing the scarred Flighter by the wrist and spinning. It was like a game his father used to play, where he held Siry by the wrist and spun him in a circle through the air. Siry used the bigger Flighter's momentum to unbalance him and spin him around. The Flighter had to run to keep from being hurled to the ground. Unfortunately for the Flighter, he couldn't stop in time. His foot went off the edge of the cliff. He fell, a horrified expression on his face, his other knee bouncing off the lip of the precipice. With a scream he disappeared.

The remaining Flighters stared, shocked at the disappearance of their leader. Siry's friend Loque took the opportunity to poleax one of them in the head. The Flighters looked at one another, then turned, and began to run.

All of them except Rena. She had reached the door and was slipping the key into the lock.

Siry charged her, slammed her into the door, then dragged her away.

The key fell from her hands as he tripped her, knocking her to the ground.

"Kill her!" shouted Twig, clutching her hurt arm.

"Take her out!" the bloodied guard yelled.

Siry fell onto Rena, his club pressed up against her throat. He could feel her body writhing under him as she struggled to escape.

"You need help?" the guard said.

"I'm fine," Siry said, shoving her back to the ground.

His face was just inches away from her. He jerked his head toward the retreating Flighters. "Follow those other guys and make sure they don't come back!"

The bloodied guard nodded. He appeared to have recovered somewhat. "He's right. Let's go." He led Loque and the others in the direction of the fleeing Flighters.

Suddenly Siry and Rena were all alone. He was lying on top of her, eyes only inches from hers.

"What's wrong with you?" he whispered. "I saved your life. I wanted to help you. And you betrayed me. You betrayed everybody in this town."

Rena laughed harshly. "Weak," she said. "Think, think, think. Talk, talk, talk. Weak."

Siry shook his head. "After all I did for you—"

"Talk?" she said. "Words? Books? No! Words nothing."

"But if you don't think, you'll never know what there is to look forward to, to plan for, to believe in."

"Eat. Sleep. Live." She paused. "Fight!" And suddenly she had a knife in her hand.

But Siry was stronger and faster than she was. He grabbed her wrist, twisted it, stripped the knife from her.

She showed no sign of surrender, though, writhing and squirming and scratching and biting. He sat up on top of her chest. He could feel the ground shaking beneath him as the heavy waves slammed the bottom of the cliff. Siry hadn't noticed until he sat up, but they were just inches from the edge now.

And then suddenly, she stopped moving. Her face went blank. She stared up at his face, her eyes empty.

"Sea trash?" she said softly. She waved her free arm carelessly over the edge of the cliff. "Trash only trash."

"You're wrong," he said. "It means something."

She waved her finger at the blue horizon. "Nothing. Out there," she said. "Nothing. Sea . . . only empty water."

She lay limp as a rag under him. His club was still pressing into her neck.

"Go," she said. "Press hard. Soon no breathe."

He stared into her green eyes. She didn't seem to be afraid at all.

"See?" she said. "Weak. Too much words."

Siry leaned a little harder on the wood, felt her neck yield. It made him feel sick. All of it. Everything that had happened today. He felt as if he could hear every crunch of bone, every split skull, every scream of pain.

When he was in the middle of the fighting, it had been just about the most exciting thing he'd ever done. But now that it was over?

His entire body started to tremble. He stood up. His legs were so weak he could barely stand.

"Go," he said.

Rena didn't speak, didn't look at him, didn't thank him. She just leaped to her feet and sprinted away. In seconds she had disappeared into the jungle.

Siry's legs gave out, and he fell to his knees. Even that seemed to take enormous effort. He stopped, hung his head down over the side of the cliff.

Below him the waves boiled and thundered on the black tangle of rocks. There was no trace of the Flighter who'd fallen into them.

After a while Siry got his strength back. He stood and looked around. Noticing the key lying on the ground, he stooped over, picked it up, stared at it.

There was writing on the side of the key, letters stamped into it that he couldn't quite make out. What did it mean?

He held the key in his hand. Then he turned toward the door. Now was his chance! He could do it. He could finally do it. He walked to the door.

Then he paused and stood in front of the large metal door without moving. This was something he had imagined for a long time. But now that he was finally here, he found himself hesitating. What if there were nothing in there? What if Rena were right? What if it were just a bunch of dark tunnels full of spiderwebs and rats and dust?

Finally, though, he extended the key, slid it into the lock.

Before he could turn it, a voice spoke from behind him.

"No."

He turned. It was his father, shaking his head.

"No, Son. Not yet. Someday, maybe. But not yet."

Siry took a breath, then another, then another. This was clearly a battle he couldn't win. Not right now. He left the key in the lock, turned and began walking back toward the village.

He could hear his father slide the key from the lock. Then they walked side by side in silence, following the path back to town. When they reached Rayne, the Flighters were all gone.

After a minute or two a guard, his shirt torn and his arms bruised, spotted Siry. He pointed. Heads turned to look. Siry wondered if he were about to get blamed for the Flighter attack.

Instead, the people on the street began to cheer.

Eight

The next day everything in Rayne seemed to have gone back to normal. No one had been killed in the Flighter attack. There were bruises and concussions and a broken bone or two, but nothing more serious. And the Flighters too had melted back into the woods, dragging away their casualties.

Siry went to school, just like normal. At school no one mentioned the attack. But there was a look on people's faces. Everyone knew that Siry's leadership and quick thinking had saved the day for the villagers. But he had also caused the attack. Everyone knew both these things. And nobody knew quite what to make of it.

As Siry walked back home after school, he felt the eyes of the town on him. But no one spoke. Not a word.

And with every step he took, Siry felt as if some kind of distance were opening up between him and the town of Rayne. It was as if he were standing on a cliff, and everyone else was standing on the other side of the chasm. Everyone, maybe, except Loque and Twig and a few of his other friends.

He felt a knot of anger building in the pit of his stomach.

When he reached home, Siry walked straight into his room, picked up his precious bag of clues that he'd found on the beach, and dumped the contents onto the floor. For the first time he saw these things as everybody else he knew must have seen them. Not clues at all. Junk. Debris. Scrap. Flotsam. Bits and pieces of unconnected, worthless, meaningless sea trash.

He gathered up his treasures, put them back in the bag, and walked slowly up the path that led to the mountain. When he reached the top of the cliff, he stood and looked out at the ocean. As far as he could see, there was nothing but the limitless blue ocean. Maybe Rena was right. Maybe life was nothing but eating and sleeping and fighting.

He opened the bag, held it up over the side of the precipice, and dumped out all his precious clues. They whirled and spun for a moment, then disappeared noiselessly into the surf.

He felt yesterday he'd come up here as a kid, and left . . . Well, not quite a man. But close. All his little childish dreams of discovering lost worlds—it was just a child's fantasy. Rena was right. The world was a harder, emptier place than he'd imagined.

After he was done, he stood there for a while. Suddenly he had the uncomfortable feeling that someone was watching him. He whirled around.

There, standing about twenty feet away, was his father. Jen Remudi had a strange, sad look on his face.

"What!" Siry said.

"I saw what you did yesterday. With the girl? Letting her go?"

Siry flushed, then shrugged.

Jen Remudi approached his son, stood next to him, and looked out at the blank, featureless horizon. "You're not wrong, Son," he said. "There is more out there."

Siry said nothing. For reasons he couldn't quite understand, he felt mad at his father.

"You wouldn't have let her go if you didn't believe there was something more, Son. Something beyond *this*." He pointed at the surf smashing fruitlessly at the black rocks.

"What are you talking about?" Siry said angrily.

"There is a great struggle going on. It takes in everything as far as the eye can see. And farther."

Siry stared mutely out at the sea.

"Come take a walk with me, Siry," his father said. "I have some things I need to tell you."

Nine

After the long conversation with his father, Siry felt his head was spinning. Travelers. Flumes. Time travel. Saint Dane. The whole thing was completely, utterly unbelievable. For fourteen years he'd been told nothing. And now all of a sudden, *this*. It seemed like just another fairy story designed to obscure the truth.

Then, at the end of the whole conversation, Jen Remudi had said to Siry that he was going to be "called away" soon. What did that even mean?

"If even half of this is true," Siry said, when his father had finally wound up his monologue, "then everybody's been lying to me for my entire life. Why?"

"No." His father shook his head. "Almost nobody here knows the big picture."

"I don't believe any of it!" Siry shouted. "It's all lies. You're just making this up to make me feel like there's more to life than this boring little village and this tiny little island."

"Son, listen, please, I'm going to be leaving soon, and I don't want to leave things between us like this.

Someday another traveler might arrive, needing your help. It is your destiny to help him. You have to believe me—"

"I don't believe anything you say," Siry said. Then he turned and ran away.

That afternoon, Siry went for a walk on the beach. As he skirted the surf, muttering to himself, he saw something glittering in the water.

Out of habit he bent to pick it up. It was a green tube, hourglass shaped, with words formed right in the clear material that it was made from. They had become so worn and pitted that it was impossible to read them. There were a lot of things he'd found over the years that could have somehow been natural objects. But not this. This was clearly made by humans. And it wasn't something that could have been made in Rayne. He'd never seen anything like it before.

The top was sealed with a soft, flexible stopper of some sort. And there was something inside, something barely visible through the scarred greenish material.

He pulled the stopper open and pulled out a piece of paper. It was folded into a tight square. He carefully opened it, trying not to tear the fragile paper.

His eyes widened. It was a map. Of Rayne . . . and much more.

Siry's hands began to tremble. He looked out to the horizon. There was nothing out there. Nothing at all . . . *was* there?

He looked back at the map, read the word at the bottom of the piece of paper. "JAKILL."

As he stared at the word, a plan began to form in his mind. He couldn't wait to tell Loque and Twig and the others. But as he thought about it, he realized that Rena was right about one thing. Ideas and books and words weren't enough. This time he wasn't just going to talk. This time he was going to *do* something.

This time, things would be different!

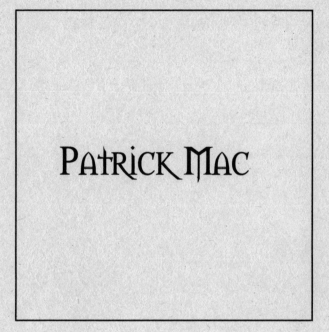

PATRICK MAC

ONE

"Curiosity. Orderliness. A passion for understanding." Patrick Mac looked around at his students. "To become a great librarian, you must have passion and a sense of mission. Because you will have to confront extraordinary challenges, challenges which—"

Jay Oh, one of his top students—but also one of his most disruptive kids—interrupted. "Yeah, like trying not to be bored to death!"

Patrick frowned. "Now, come on, Jay. I'm making a serious point here," he said. He tried to look as stern as he could.

But the truth was, he sometimes wondered if Jay wasn't right. Patrick loved teaching, loved working as a researcher in the world's most important library. And yet sometimes he wondered—was this it? Was this all he'd been put on earth to do? He was good at his job. Very good. But sometimes it seemed like poking around in computers full of ancient facts and figures—or teaching young people how to poke around in computers—just wasn't all that important.

It wasn't like the fate of the universe depended on whether you could dig up some old piece of information. He was talking to the class about having a sense of mission. But did he really feel that way himself? He used to think he did. But now he wasn't so sure. Maybe he was saying all this to convince himself.

As Patrick tried to refocus on the point he'd been making, there was a knock on the door of his classroom. The door opened a crack. Patrick could see one bright green eye looking through the door. There was only one person in the building who had eyes quite that color. It was the director of the New York Public Library herself.

"Mr. Mac?" The director's voice came through the door. "A word, if I may?"

Patrick took a deep breath. The air in the office of the director of the New York Public Library had a special smell to it—the smell of ancient books, of history, of human achievement. For five thousand years the building in which Patrick sat had been devoted to recording and keeping all the knowledge of humankind. And to sit in the office of the director herself! Well, it was a great feeling.

The director was a small, wizened woman with long white hair. She gave Patrick a wincing smile. "We have a problem."

Patrick Mac sat up straighter. Had he done something wrong? He had been a teacher at the School of the New York Public Library for several years now and was still one of the junior members of the library staff. Despite having a natural talent for the work, he was frequently made to feel his inexperience by the older members of the organization. "I'm sorry," he said. "What did I do?"

"You? Who said anything about you?"

"Well, I assumed—"

The director cut him off with a wave of her hand. "Don't assume." She pointed at the rows of books on the shelves of her large, wood-paneled office. Most of the library's real books were kept in rooms deep underground, but a certain group was on display in the director's office. "Our collection contains many of the most valuable, rare, and magnificent books in the world. The Gutenberg Bible, the Nag Hammadi scrolls, the early Shakespeare folios—I could go on and on."

Patrick Mac knew this. Of course, all the books had been copied as digital images, and the information they contained was stored in computers. But the books had a value beyond the information they contained. They were an actual, physical connection to the entire history of human beings on Earth.

"Several books have gone missing, Patrick," the director said.

"Missing?" Patrick frowned. "How is that possible?"

"They've been stolen."

Patrick's eyes widened. Stolen! The word itself had an old-fashioned sound to it. People didn't steal things anymore. Sure, occasionally a kid would grab somebody's lunch as a prank. But this was a world of bounty, a world in which no one was poor, no one wanted for anything. There was literally no point in stealing. "But . . . why?"

The director shook her head. "I was hoping you would be able to tell us."

Patrick swallowed. "Do you think that I—"

"Don't be ridiculous!" the director said irritably.

"Then why me?"

"Two reasons. A long time ago, back when breaking the law was common, there were people who solved crimes."

"Detectives!" Patrick said excitedly. He'd gone through a phase when he was a boy, reading ancient books about crime solvers. "Sleuths, private eyes, investigators—"

"You don't have to try to impress me with all the words you know, Patrick," the director said sharply.

Patrick cleared his throat. "Yes, yes, of course. I'm sorry."

"You have distinguished yourself as a person with an unusual ability to dig up information."

"Thank you, Director."

"That skill may—I repeat, *may*—be of use to us at some point."

"Wow!"

The Director narrowed her eyes. She was famous for her dislike of emotional displays.

"I'm sorry!" Patrick said. Then he frowned. "You said there were two reasons you wanted me to investigate the theft."

"I did."

Patrick waited.

"I'm sorry to be the one to tell you this," the director said. "But the thief appears to be one of your students."

"That's not possible!" Patrick said.

"I'm afraid it is. As you know, your students have

pass codes that allow them entry to certain areas of the library. The thief was able to alter his or her code so as to enter and exit the building without being identified. But what the student apparently didn't realize was that every pass code also contains information about what group or organization they are connected to. The group code points straight at the class you teach."

"What about video? There are vid scanners in the library, aren't there?"

"Of course."

"Then we should be able to see who it is."

"Unfortunately, however, we are not."

"Why not?"

"There have been certain . . . alterations to the hologram video files. The identity of the thief has been masked."

Masked? How was that possible? Patrick decided not to pursue the matter. "Then what about the books? The thief must be doing something with them, right? Giving them to someone, storing them, selling them, sharing them . . ."

"No."

Patrick looked at the director curiously. "Then . . ."

"They're burning them."

A wave of horror flooded through him. Burning books! There wasn't a book in the library that wasn't at least two thousand years old. It had been eons since books were actually printed. Even the most trivial books were important artifacts of earlier times. "But that's sick!" he said.

The director nodded.

"So . . . I guess you want me to investigate?"

The director looked puzzled for a moment. "Oh!" she said. "My goodness, no. You've quite misunderstood me."

"But I thought you said—"

"I simply called you here today to inform you that a police investigator would be coming to your class today. His name is Sergeant Lane. I wanted to make certain that you extend him every courtesy."

Patrick's excitement evaporated. For a moment there, he thought she'd wanted him to take on an exciting assignment—investigator! Sleuth! Detective! But apparently not.

"Oh," Patrick said.

"You're disappointed," the director said.

Patrick sighed. "No, I just . . . Well, when you started talking about investigators . . ."

"I understand." The director smiled kindly. "You're an excellent teacher and a good librarian. We appreciate that. But let's not get carried away."

Patrick saw that it was almost time for his class to start. "Well, I'd better get going."

"Keep your eyes open, Patrick."

"I will."

Two

Patrick walked slowly down the hallway to the elevator that took him down to sublevel twenty-six, where class was about to start. He'd been teaching for about five years now. It was good work, really it was. He liked the kids, he enjoyed the work. But still, he kept feeling like something was missing. There was no excitement, no feeling that anything really huge was at stake.

His students were good kids. Sometimes he felt as if they didn't need him at all. They all did their work. They logged on to their computers, and the computers fed them assignments at a rate that was determined by tests that were administered and graded by the computers. Sure, Patrick lectured every day. Sure, he tried to help the kids when they had problems that the teaching programs couldn't get them past.

But really. Did the kids need him? Sometimes he felt as if he were nothing but a high-class babysitter.

He needed a challenge!

But *what*? He sometimes wished that he could have been born a few thousand years ago, back when bad things actually happened, back when people had real problems that demanded courage and strength and tenacity. Today everything was safe and easy and perfect.

And boring.

As he approached the class, he saw a man standing by the door. The man's clothes looked normal—except for a thin gold band on each shoulder. It reminded Patrick of the gold braid that soldiers and police had worn years and years ago. As he got closer, Patrick saw that the gold band was formed of tiny numerals—a row of nines.

"My goodness!" Patrick said. "You're from Unit Nine!"

The man turned and smiled confidently. He had a smooth, handsome face with a square jaw and brown eyes. He looked like an actor from the vids. "Guilty as charged," he said, winking. "Sergeant Eric Lane, at your service."

"Unit Nine!" Patrick couldn't believe it. The vids were full of stories about the supersecret Unit 9 of the Global Police Force. "I always assumed Unit Nine was totally fictional."

"You're not the only one," Sergeant Lane said. "We like it that way. Keeps the villains on their toes." The Unit 9 investigator threw a mock punch, stopping only inches from Patrick's face.

"Whoa!" Patrick said, flinching. "For a second I thought you were going to do me harm."

Sergeant Lane laughed genially. He had a rich baritone voice. "I trust you've been briefed?"

"Briefed?" Patrick was momentarily confused. "Oh, sure. The director told me you were coming."

"Out*standing*!" Sergeant Lane said. Then he pointed at the room. "Let's get the show on the road, shall we?"

Patrick walked into the class and said, "Everyone take your places."

There were slightly more than a dozen kids in the class, seven boys and seven girls, all of them around fifteen years of age. They grumbled good-naturedly as they sat.

Patrick explained to the students that they had a special guest for the day, Sergeant Lane from Unit 9. This caused a stir in the class.

Sergeant Lane stood at the front of the class and said, "Well, I'm going to ask you some questions. A couple of items have gone missing from the library, and I've been tasked to recover them." He looked around the room expectantly. Patrick wondered what he was waiting for. He assumed that the investigator would be talking to the students individually. "So . . . anybody, uh, anybody know what I'm talking about? Anybody aware of some missing items?"

The class looked at him blankly.

Sergeant Lane had seemed very confident at first. But now he seemed somewhat uncomfortable. "Hm? Anybody? Anybody want to help me out?"

"What's missing?" said Em Stickler, a willowy girl with short blond hair.

Sergeant Lane cleared his throat. "Not at liberty to say, I'm afraid." He looked around the room. "Anybody?"

Patrick Mac was feeling a little puzzled. He'd read a lot of ancient books about crime solving. And no detective he'd ever read about would have done things the way Sergeant Lane was doing them.

"Well . . . if you don't tell us what's missing," said Jay Oh, "then how can we tell you if we know what happened to it?"

Sergeant Lane looked at Patrick. "Help me out here, Patrick," he said. "These kids don't seem like they've got a helping attitude."

Patrick smiled nervously. "Don't you think it would be a good idea to question them individually?" he said. "Then you could compare their stories and see if they add up."

Sergeant Lane scratched his face uneasily. "Uh—well, yes, sure, that's probably—yes, let's go ahead and do that." He looked around the room as though searching for a spot to question the students.

"There's an empty classroom next door. Maybe I could bring them in there one by one?"

"Out*standing*!" Sergeant Lane said. "I'll be next door then."

He wheeled and walked out of the room.

The students looked at one another with perplexed expressions on their faces.

After the class was over and he'd questioned each of the students, Sergeant Lane said to Patrick, "Well, I thought that went really well! Really well indeed!" Patrick noticed that the detective was sweating heavily, as if he were nervous about something.

"What did you find out?"

"Find out?" The investigator blinked. "Uh . . .

well . . . not much." He showed off his straight, white teeth. "Can't expect too much on the first round of questioning though."

"Oh, okay." Patrick was a little surprised. In the crime novels he'd read, the detective usually found out all kinds of stuff when they talked to suspects.

"Good call on the—uh—the separate room thing. I never would have thought of that."

Patrick frowned. "Really? How do you usually do it?"

Sergeant Lane looked at the floor uncomfortably. "Actually?" He cleared his throat. "Actually this is my first major investigation."

Patrick was a little surprised. "How long have you been in Unit Nine?"

"Twelve years next month."

Patrick stared. "And you've never investigated anything?"

Sergeant Lane looked insulted. "Of course I have! It's just this is my first *major* case."

"I'm relieved to hear that. I thought—"

"In fact, I've made *nine* arrests!" The investigator nodded sagely. "I'll never forget my first, though.'" He narrowed his eyes thoughtfully. "Six-year-old boy. Stole a communicator from his teacher. I put in three months on that case. Very instructive. Very instructive indeed."

Patrick tried not to look appalled. Someone was stealing priceless volumes from the library and the best investigator they could find had never investigated anything more complex than a kid who stole a minor electronic gizmo?

"Of course," Sergeant Lane said, "I've also completed

several excellent simulations. There was an out*standing* one where I had to crack a ring of gunrunners who were smuggling weapons to terrorists in a . . ." His smile faded. "Of course, that simulation was several thousand years old. Since we don't really have weapons anymore. Or terrorists. Or smugglers. Or . . ."

Suddenly Patrick was not feeling very hopeful about the detective's ability to solve the crime. If he hadn't known better, he'd have thought this was a joke. "But you do feel confident you can solve this crime?"

The sergeant smiled broadly. "Unit Nine always gets their man," he said. His self-possession seemed to be coming back now.

"Great," Patrick said. He hesitated. There was still a question that had been bothering him. "The library has surveillance vid scanners. Didn't the scanners capture the theft on video?"

The detective looked at him sternly. "That's information I really can't release to you. Strictly need-to-know."

"I mean, if the theft is on video, you should be able to avoid all this. Right?"

Sergeant Lane said nothing. He was looking increasingly annoyed.

Patrick couldn't help himself though. He was really curious to know what was going on. "You think it would be helpful if I spoke to the students myself?"

Sergeant Lane held up one hand, palm out. "Okay, okay, stop right there, Pat. I know you're eager to help. But you need to let the professionals handle this."

Patrick hated being called "Pat." "I just thought—"

The investigator's face hardened. Patrick couldn't

help thinking that the expression looked like something the investigator had practiced a lot in a mirror. "Do me a favor, Pat. Don't think. Leave the thinking to me."

Patrick felt his brow furrowing.

Sergeant Lane whirled and began walking briskly off down the hallway.

"Um . . . Sergeant?" Patrick called.

The policeman stopped, turned.

"That's a dead end," Patrick said. "You want to go in the other direction."

"I knew that!" Sergeant Lane said, marching back the other way. His shoes clicked sharply on the floor until he was gone.

THREE

Later that afternoon Patrick knocked on the door of the director's office.

"Ma'am?" he said, peeking around the door frame. "Sorry to bother you. But . . . well, I met with the investigator today. And I have to tell you, I wasn't that impressed."

The director looked away from the hologram screen she'd been studying and frowned. "He seemed quite professional."

"Yes," Patrick said. "Until he actually starts working."

"He's from Unit Nine! I'm sure he has his methods."

"If he does, I can't see them," Patrick said.

"What exactly do you want?" the director said, narrowing her eyes.

"I want to help with the investigation."

The director frowned. "Patrick, you have a lot on your plate. On top of your teaching load and your duties at the library? No, I'm afraid I just can't authorize it."

"But—"

The director looked at the clock projected in the air

above her desk. "Aren't you supposed to be auditing the new cataloging program right now?"

"Yes, ma'am."

"Then you'd better get cracking. The project is already severely behind schedule." The director looked back at her screen, dismissing Patrick without saying a word.

Patrick closed the door quietly and slunk back to his work space. The public library was a very old organization, very traditional. There was a way to do everything. Authority was respected. Lines were not crossed. You did as you were told.

He slumped down in his chair and sighed. This whole situation just wasn't right. He'd seen the detective at work. The guy just didn't know what he was doing. It was no fault of his own, really. There just wasn't any crime to investigate anymore, so a police officer just didn't ever have a chance to learn his business.

As Patrick was musing about the situation, two of his students walked in—Em and Jay. "Okay," Jay said, "so that guy from Unit Nine was a total joke, huh?"

Jay was by far the most sarcastic kid in his class.

As a symbol of authority to the students, Patrick felt obliged to defend the detective. "Well, I'm sure he's going to get to the bottom of this matter," he said.

"Yeah, right." Jay snorted.

"I was a little confused too, I must admit," said Em. She and Jay were the top students at the School of the New York Public Library. But their personalities couldn't have been more different. Where Jay was abrasive and quick to argue, Em was soft spoken and easygoing.

"How so?" Patrick asked.

"Well . . ." She seemed to be trying to find a tactful way to say something. "He just asked a lot of vague, pointless questions. And I couldn't quite figure out what he was driving at."

"What she's saying," Jay said, "is the guy is an idiot."

"Now, hold on," Patrick said. "He's a member of Unit Nine. I'm sure—"

"All I'm saying," Em said, "is that I was confused. I never even figured out what he was looking for."

"Yeah," Jay said. "What's missing? What's the big deal here?"

"I'm not really sure that I'm supposed to say," Patrick said.

Jay rolled his eyes.

"Maybe we can help," Em said.

"I can only say," Patrick replied, "that something has been stolen from the library. And it looks like somebody in your class took it."

"It had to be a book, right?" Jay said. "Yes? Right? Did somebody steal the Gutenberg Bible?"

"I can't say."

Em's eyes widened. "Somebody stole the Gutenberg Bible? Really?"

"Don't be silly," Patrick said.

"Then what?" Jay said. "First edition of *The Sun Also Rises*? Jefferson's draft of the Declaration of Independence?"

"No, it was just some books."

"Aha!" Jay said. "So it *was* a book!"

Patrick flushed. "I really can't say."

"We'd just like to help," Em said. "That's all we're saying."

"Sure," Patrick said.

"The more we know, the more we can help."

Patrick felt as if he were playing the director's role now. "It's being handled," he said. "Don't worry about it."

Em and Jay looked at each other skeptically.

"I've got lots of work to do," Patrick said.

"Okay, okay, okay!" Jay said. "We can see when we're not wanted."

The two left Patrick's work space. He expanded the hologram screen and started running the audit program. But he just couldn't concentrate. It was routine, unchallenging work. He didn't want to admit it, but he was bored stiff.

Finally he looked around to make sure nobody was watching. Then he spoke to the screen. "Pull up all library security files."

The computer told him that he didn't have authorization. No matter what the older members of the staff said about his inexperience, it was generally acknowledged that if you wanted to find information, Patrick Mac was your man. There was no corner of the NYPL's system that Patrick couldn't reach. It didn't take him three minutes to find a route into the library's security files.

"Pull up security cameras."

Several views of the library appeared, floating in the air above his desk.

"Review for unauthorized use of books in the past thirty days."

The screen flashed the names of three books. Under each was a list of dates, times, and camera views.

"Show sequential views for the first book," Patrick said.

A view of a room full of books appeared in the air. For a moment nothing happened. Then a figure strolled into the room, took a book, and walked out of the room. Patrick blinked. *Wait a minute!* he thought. *That's not possible!*

A second view popped up, this time showing a large hallway. A woman Patrick didn't recognize appeared. Patrick breathed a sigh of relief. That was more like it. A real person. And it wasn't a student from his class. But then, to his shock, the original figure appeared again, walking briskly down the hallway.

"Fast forward!" Patrick said.

The same figure appeared in a rapid succession of hologram videos, zipping through the library at high speed with the stolen volume under its arm.

"Show all," Patrick said, "fast speed."

Again the same figure appeared. In each of the three vids, the figure stole a book, took it out the front door onto Fifth Avenue. And set it on fire.

"Freeze!"

In the last frame of the most recent video, the projection froze. Patrick stared at the image for a long time. This didn't make a bit of sense.

The figure with the book tucked under its arm wasn't human. In fact, it wasn't even real. It was a cartoon.

Based on his study of history and art, Patrick identified the figure in the video as being a cartoon that would have been drawn somewhere in the twentieth century. It was a squat, bowlegged creature with a mischievous face and silly-looking tuft that might have been feathers sticking up on top of its head.

"View three hundred sixty degrees," he said.

The hologram scanners in the library were capable of filming an object from any direction. They weren't like ancient cameras—a lens stuck on the front of a sensing device. Instead, they were small sensors planted throughout a room that stored image data on everything in the room. As a result, images could be assembled by computer and viewed from almost any angle. They also scanned all frequencies from infrared to ultraviolet, so they could record images even in total darkness.

The image of the room rotated slowly in the air. Strangely, the cartoon figure seemed absolutely three dimensional, appearing just as solid and real as everything else in the room.

"Somebody has hacked the security files," Patrick whispered. Somehow every single image of the real thief had been replaced by this silly-looking cartoon figure.

"Run hack scan?" the voice of the computer said.

"Yes," Patrick said.

There was a long pause. Then a message flashed on the screen. "No hack found."

"Run a level-six scan," Patrick said.

"I am required to inform you that a level-six scan will require unusual resources from the central processing—"

"I know all that," Patrick snapped. "Do it anyway."

"Director-level authorization required."

Patrick took a deep breath. He knew a way of invoking the director's authorization. The computer was supposed to only accept the director's own voice. But Patrick had stored a work-around. Just in case.

His hands felt shaky. This wasn't something he could do by speaking to the computer. This had to be typed in. Hardly any librarians bothered to learn how to type anymore. They just talked to the computer.

Patrick brought up the hologram keyboard and typed in a series of commands.

"Level-six hack scan authorized," the computer said. The lights dimmed suddenly and the hologram projection shrank to a tiny, bright point in the air, then blinked off. Patrick's eyes widened. He had never run a level-six hack scan before. They really weren't kidding when they said it ate up a lot of resources. The whole building was powering down. Patrick swallowed. This was not good. Somebody was going to notice what he'd just done. And when they did, Patrick was going to get in big trouble.

The lights slowly went back up, but the projection remained dark. Patrick counted off the seconds. Five, ten, fifteen, twenty . . . thirty!

Suddenly the projection popped up again.

"No hacks found," the calm voice of the computer said.

"Not possible," Patrick said. "Somebody altered the video!"

"No," said the computer. "All three videos are unaltered."

"Come on!" Patrick said. "That's a cartoon with a

fringy doohickey on its head. It's not possible. It's not real."

"I'm not sure how to respond," the computer said.

"Of course you aren't," Patrick said. "That's because you're a stupid computer."

"I'm not sure how to respond," the computer said.

"Someone hacked the computer," Patrick said. "Somebody *really* good."

The image of the cartoon figure hovered over Patrick's work space, leering right at Patrick's face.

Well, he thought, *no wonder Unit 9 got called in.* This really was puzzling. It was too bad that Unit 9 didn't seem to know what they were doing.

He looked at the names of the three volumes that had been stolen from the library. "Run a correlation on the three books," he said.

"All three books are first editions, written and printed in the early twentieth century in the United States of America. They are generally considered to be among the most popular children's books of their period."

"Anything else?"

"Each is printed on paper made of cotton fiber and contains more than one hundred fifty and fewer than two hundred pages. Their average sentence length lies between—"

"Okay, okay, okay, that's enough," Patrick said. He thought for a minute. "Expand the group. Assume that the thief is going to steal another book. What would the next book be?"

"Assuming the factors mentioned earlier are decisive in the thief's decision-making process, there is an eighty-nine percent probability that the next theft will be *The Wonderful Wizard of Oz* by L. Frank Baum."

"Where is that book located?"

"Floor sub thirty-nine, section E, room nineteen, shelf two hundred thirty-one."

"Is there any pattern to the times of the thefts?"

"All took place between seven and eight o'clock on either a Wednesday or a Thursday night."

Patrick raised an eyebrow. Wednesday. That was tonight!

He drummed his fingers on his desk. Finally he spoke. "Close window. Store all video data in a file called 'My Skiing Trip to Colorado.' Falsify the date to fit my last trip to Colorado. Erase all transactions from this session."

"That is not authorized."

"Do it anyway."

"I am not sure how to respond."

"Override. Utilize key sequence nine-seven-seven-one-three."

There was a brief pause. Then the computer said, "Transaction files erased. Session terminated."

Patrick stood. His hands were trembling.

What am I doing? he thought. *This is crazy! This is not me. This is not me at all.*

Then his legs got wobbly for a moment, and he had to sit down.

He sat silently for a while. He could hear a roaring noise in his ears, and his vision started going gray. He put his head between his legs.

After a minute his vision started to clear and the

roaring noise went away. He looked up at the clock: 6:45! How had it gotten so late?

As he stood, a small bell chimed on his comm. He took his silver communicator off his belt and looked at the tiny screen. It was the director calling. Red letters flashed on the screen. URGENT. URGENT. URGENT. Patrick took a deep breath. *What do I do?* After a moment he thumbed the off button.

"Oops," he said. "I guess I turned off my communicator. By accident."

His heart was pounding as he jumped up and hurried down the hallway to the elevator. He stopped, turned, ran back to the office.

Sitting on his desk was a small red band of flexible material, a collar he had just bought for his cat, Earnest. The old collar had gotten worn and frayed, so he'd bought a new one. He stuck the collar in his pocket, then turned and ran out of the room again.

I can't believe I'm doing this, he thought. *I really can't believe it.*

FOUR

The upper floors of the New York Public Library had a grand, ancient feel that reflected the age and importance of the institution. But once you got down into the area underground where all the books were stored, it became as bland, featureless, and cramped as a warehouse. Each low-ceilinged room contained row on row of shelves crammed with ancient books.

The air was cool and bitter smelling. Under normal circumstances books decomposed over time. But here the highly filtered air contained chemicals that suppressed the molds, bacteria, and insects that would otherwise eventually eat and destroy the old paper. In this environment books could theoretically last forever. Even the light was kept intentionally dim, only coming on when people entered a room, so that the rays wouldn't degrade the paper or the bindings of the books. In rooms where especially valuable books were stored, the light was a creepy red color, the lower wavelengths being less damaging to paper.

Patrick had come to love the odd smell of the stacks,

the dim light, the cramped conditions. But now that he suspected a crime was about to be committed, the stacks seemed a little frightening. All of these books were kept mostly for historical reasons, not because they were sources of information. If you just wanted to read them, it was much more convenient to pull them up on the holo screen So many parts of the library might go years without anybody entering them.

Patrick felt very alone.

He walked swiftly through the stacks toward room 191. It was called a "room," but it was as big as a catchball field. It took a while, but eventually Patrick found it. The door whooshed open. On the other side of it was total inky darkness.

Patrick entered. The dim red lights in the section of the room closest to him switched on. He began walking slowly through the stacks. Wherever he went, the lights switched on—switching off a few strides behind him— so that he walked in a pool of bloodred light, while around him stretched acres of silent blackness. His shoes moved silently on the soft floor.

As he walked past the ends of the shelves, small screens lit up, giving him the LC numbers of the shelves. Finally, after what seemed an enormously long walk, he reached the correct shelf. He had to hurry! It was almost seven.

Standing in the pool of eerie red light, he pulled the cat collar out of his pocket and felt it with his fingers. There was a slightly thicker part right in the middle. Like any normal pet collar, it had a tracking device for recovering wandering pets. He could feel the tracking chip with his fingers. He tore the cat collar in half with his teeth, then pushed and prodded until the tracking device came out. It was a small, flat gray disk.

Using the writing stylus from his comm, he jammed the little gray disk down into the spine of the book. There was a ripping sound as he forced it through the old binding material. It made him feel almost sick to desecrate the book. But it was all for a good purpose, right? He doubted anyone had touched this particular volume in centuries. Maybe not even for a thousand years. Who'd notice?

A small, irritating bell began to chime. "Alert, alert, alert," a computer voice said, emanating from the ceiling. "Library employee Patrick Mac, you have improperly handled volume number seven-nine-four-six-three-dash-one. Please have it repaired immediately."

"Noted," Patrick said. "Now could you please be quiet."

"Yes, Patrick Mac."

The silence that followed felt numb, deafening. Patrick looked at the book. There was a definite small lump in the spine, where the pet locator chip was situated. He hoped the thief wouldn't notice.

Patrick retreated four or five shelves away from the book and sat on the floor, his back against a shelf. He situated himself so that he could peer out through the gap between two rows of books. He could see the entrance to the row of shelves where *The Wonderful Wizard of Oz* was located. But unless the thief was looking right at him, Patrick would be impossible to see.

He sighed. There was nothing to do now but

wait. Would the thief even come? The computer had predicted that this was the next volume that would be stolen. But what if the computer was wrong? He'd defaced an ancient historical object . . . and all for nothing!

He looked around. In the red light that had followed him to where he sat, everything looked strange and menacing, like something out of a horror vid. He felt nervous and shaky.

Suddenly, after he'd been sitting for a minute, something occurred to him: If the thief did come, the red light would be a dead giveaway that Patrick was sitting there.

He had a choice. He could leave the room and rely on the tracking device. Or he could sit in the darkness and wait.

He decided he'd better wait. If the thief discovered the tracking device, then he would have defaced the book for nothing. And he'd have no more idea who the thief was than he'd had before.

"Turn off lights," he said.

The pool of red light disappeared. Deep underground, with no windows and no access to light, room 191 of the New York Public Library became as dark as a tomb. There was literally not a single ray of light in the entire place.

Patrick felt a shiver run down his spine. For the umpteenth time in the past few hours, he wondered why he was doing this. He had never been a brave person. When he was a boy, he'd known kids who were always taking risks, climbing walls, exploring tunnels, falling and breaking their arms. But not Patrick. He'd always been careful, thoughtful, calm—even a little timid. It was no accident he'd ended up a librarian and teacher. He felt safe and secure when he was reading, studying, holed up in a small place where he could study and think.

He was not a tracking-down-criminals kind of guy.

He sat in the dark, listening to his heartbeat. *Ka-kshhhh, ka-kshhhh, ka-kshhhh.* Every moment or two he considered standing up and walking out of the room. Everyone was telling him to leave it to the pro from Unit 9. But there was something about the crime that offended him. *Burning books!* When you burned a book, you were spitting in the face of knowledge, of understanding, of history. A person who burned a book was pretty much capable of anything.

But that man from Unit 9? Jay Oh was right—the guy was just plain stupid. And besides, Sergeant Lane probably didn't understand what these books represented. This was the inherited knowledge of all mankind! If this wasn't stopped here, where *would* it stop? Only a librarian could really understand just how important this was.

Suddenly in the distance Patrick heard a sound. The soft whoosh of an automatic door opening. For a moment a shaft of pale light cut through the gloom. As quickly as it had appeared, it was gone.

Patrick frowned. If the thief had entered the room, the lights should be coming on. But they weren't.

Maybe it wasn't the thief after all. Maybe someone had walked by and the door had opened automatically.

Or maybe the thief had started to enter, but somehow sensed Patrick's presence. There was no way to know. Whoever it was, was gone.

Patrick took his comm off his belt to check the time. He had forgotten about turning it off. He switched it back on. The urgent message from the director was still blinking. He erased it without listening, then looked at the clock. It was past eight. Maybe the thief wasn't coming. Patrick put the comm back on his belt.

Suddenly the hairs on the back of his neck stood up. He heard something! A soft, stealthy scraping sound. Footsteps!

But . . . why weren't the lights coming on? Whoever it was, they were getting closer. The thing Patrick couldn't figure out, though, was how the thief could see. Obviously they didn't want anyone to see *them*. But if no one could see them, then how could they see where they were going?

Patrick's heart started beating faster as the furtive footsteps grew closer and closer. Then something occurred to him. If he could log into the security channel, he could watch the person on the tiny screen of his comm.

He pulled out his comm, used his writing stylus to navigate quickly through the menus until he reached the security sensors. Within seconds a ghostly image appeared on his screen. The sensors didn't use light here. Because there was none. But that didn't matter. The scanners could pick up infrared light. The infrared image didn't look like the normal visible-light vids though. It had a ghostly, transparent quality.

He stared at the screen in disbelief. Walking toward

him was the silly-looking cartoon character he'd seen on the security footage before.

He had assumed that the security files had been altered in the computer's memory after the theft occurred. But apparently the thief had managed to alter the program so that his or her own image was being obscured in real time, replacing the real image with that of the crazy cartoon figure.

Closer and closer the cartoon figure came. Occasionally it paused, looked around suspiciously, then continued stealthily forward. On its face was the same taunting smirk as before.

Finally it stopped. *Yes!* Patrick thought. *The computer prediction was right!* The cartoon figure had stopped at the row of shelves where *The Wonderful Wizard of Oz* was situated.

The cartoon figure stood for a moment, head cocked, as though listening. Then suddenly it darted forward and grabbed the book.

Patrick couldn't see anything but the tiny image on the screen. He realized that if the thief moved fast enough, he might escape without Patrick being able to see his face.

"Lights on full!" Patrick shouted.

Instead of the puddle of red light that had followed him before, the entire ceiling lit up, a bright, blinding white. For a moment Patrick could barely see, his eyes overloaded with the brightness.

The thief's footsteps resounded loudly. He was sprinting toward the far door.

As his eyes adjusted, Patrick jumped to his feet. To

his horror he realized that after sitting for over an hour in the same position, one of his feet had fallen asleep. He had no sensation in his left leg and no ability to hold himself upright.

As he began to fall, he grabbed wildly at the nearest bookshelf. For a moment he thought it would support his weight. But the shelf began to teeter. With a crash Patrick fell to the floor, the shelf smashing down on top of him.

He fell just far enough into the aisle to spot the retreating figure of the thief. He was relieved to see it was a real flesh-and-blood person and not a cartoon. But other than that, he couldn't make out any features. The thief was dressed in the baggy white clothes that were fashionable among kids that year. The clothes revealed nothing of the person underneath. He couldn't even tell if it was a boy or a girl. And the thief's head was covered with something that obscured his or her hair.

Hearing the loud crash, the thief turned to look back. Patrick realized then how the thief had managed to see in the dark. He or she was wearing a black mask made of some kind of smooth, glassy material. Patrick recognized it as a night-vision mask of the sort worn by soldiers and police many hundreds of years ago. A friend's father had owned one when Patrick was a kid. They used to play games with it in the dark. It was capable of light amplification, infrared detection, sonar, micro- and radio-wave imaging, and other things he had long forgotten about. When you were wearing it, you could see anything, anytime, anywhere.

And no one could see your face.

Patrick pushed himself to his knees, shrugging the heavy shelf of books off his back. By the time he looked up again, the thief was gone.

"Nice try, pal," Patrick said, smiling.

He picked up his comm, pulled up the security menu. "Theft in progress," he said. "Seal all exits. Stop all elevators."

He smiled triumphantly. The thief believed he'd thought of everything. But he hadn't bargained on Patrick Mac!

"Security malfunction," the comm said back to him.

Patrick's face fell. "What!"

"Security malfunction," the comm said again. Then a list of all kinds of doors and sensors and locks began scrolling rapidly down the screen, the word "FAILED" appearing in red letters next to each one.

Patrick punched his fist angrily into his palm.

He pushed himself slowly to his feet.

"Urgent message, Patrick," the comm said.

Patrick stumbled slowly forward. Feeling was starting to come back in his foot.

"Urgent message, Patrick."

Patrick sighed loudly. He'd failed completely. He felt so stupid. The thief had thought of everything! And now the director was about to reprimand him. Maybe even fire him.

"Urgent message, Patrick."

"Okay," Patrick mumbled.

"Urgent message, Patrick."

"Okay, okay, *what*? Who's the message from?"

"Pet Tracker Technologies wishes to inform you that

your cat, Earnest, has escaped," the comm said. "Would you like me to track it for you?"

Patrick grinned and began hobbling as rapidly as he could toward the distant door of room 191.

Earnest? No, Earnest was safe and sound back in his apartment.

"Why, yes," Patrick said, smiling. "Yes, I would like that very much. Forward the tracking data to my comm, please."

FIVE

The vast majority of what was once New York City was now underground. There were remnants of the ancient city left—the lions outside the New York Public Library, the silver-clad Empire State Building, other monuments and buildings. But the city was mostly a maze of tunnels and underground chambers that extended hundreds of feet deep and contained thousands of miles of corridors.

For the most part the underground was as bright and cheerfully lit as the outdoors. Beautiful iridescent murals covered the walls, and the nearly unlimited power sources available to society meant that being underground never meant feeling as if you were in a cave.

Well . . . *almost* never.

For about an hour Patrick had been tracking the signal from the cat collar he'd stuffed into the spine of *The Wonderful Wizard of Oz*. And during that time the thief had been winding deeper and deeper into the tunnels that composed the city. And now he was beginning to find himself in parts of the city that were, well, pretty cavelike.

They had passed through the sections where most people lived and worked, then into the deeper, darker Maintenance Sector. M-Sector, as it was known, was an old shadow world whose roots went back thousands of years. Back when working underground wasn't easy or cheap the way it was today. Down here was where the pumps and air ducts and water systems, as well as the geothermal power units that supplied much of the city's power were located.

Huge metal bracing held up the ceilings of the chambers he passed through, many of which were lit by ancient bulbs whose flickering light threw dark shadows into the corners of every room.

Some of the people Patrick passed in M-Sector clearly worked on the huge machinery that supported the city. But many other people seemed furtive or listless, their clothes dirty and unfashionable, their eyes clouded with fear or anger or mistrust. Patrick was not used to seeing people like that. It made him nervous. Some of the people he passed eyed him as though they were considering attacking him.

As Patrick entered one of the vast, dim, echoing chambers, he spotted the thief again for the first time. The thief was hurrying along, head down, not looking backward. Patrick still couldn't make out who it was. The thief was no longer wearing the night-vision mask, but instead, one of the large, floppy hats that were currently in fashion, still hiding his or her face and the color and length of hair.

"Hey!" Patrick yelled.

Without looking back, the thief ducked through a small door on the side of the large chamber.

Patrick had noticed that here in M-Section the tracer signal was starting to break up, sometimes disappearing from the screen on his comm. Something to do with the large amounts of electromagnetic energy produced by the generators down here, he supposed.

Patrick broke into a run. The chamber was at least two hundred meters long. By the time he'd covered a hundred meters, the little red circle on his comm screen had flashed a few times and then disappeared.

He was out of breath when he reached the door. It was made of heavy steel, surrounded by thumb-size rivets and covered in chipped greenish paint.

VALVE CHAMBER 7

DANGER!

AUTHORIZED PERSONNEL ONLY
NYC DEPT OF ENVIRONMENTAL PROTECTION

The sign on the door was so scarred and worn that it was barely readable. From the looks of it, this part of the tunnel system was almost certainly thousands of years old.

Patrick twisted the massive steel handle and pushed the door open with a deep groan. What he found on the other side amazed him.

Darkness. It was the first time he'd ever seen real

darkness in the city. It wasn't that there was no light at all, but the light was so dim and flickering that for a moment he almost couldn't see anything. Then he realized what the source of the light was. Fire! Scattered here and there throughout the tunnel were tiny fires.

The chamber he had entered was a long tunnel, maybe ten meters high, carved from solid rock. The floor was wet, the walls oozing and dripping. A thick acrid haze of smoke filled the tunnel.

The thief was nowhere to be seen. Not that Patrick could have seen much of anybody in this smoky gloom.

For a moment Patrick hesitated. But then a voice inside his head said, "You have to find the book!" Patrick couldn't ignore it. He stepped forward a few feet, trying to see better.

Behind him, the door slammed shut with a great groaning *boooooooooom*.

"Hey!" Patrick called. The sound echoed loudly, repeating and repeating before finally dying away.

As his eyes adjusted, Patrick suddenly realized, to his shock, that he was not alone. Scattered here and there were small clusters of people. They were sitting around the tiny fires. Some of them seemed to be cooking things over the flames.

Patrick felt a sick sensation run through him. Who *were* these people? There were legends, of course, about people who lived in the deeper reaches of the tunnels. They were called "roaches." The stories were crazy and unbelievable. People said that roaches stole, fought, killed—that they even *ate* one another! Patrick had always believed that these were just stories told to scare kids. But now, looking around at the huddled figures in the chamber, he wasn't so sure.

"Hey!" Patrick called again, his voice cracking a little.

Hundreds of pairs of eyes turned toward him, glinting in the firelight. Every single pair of eyes seemed to be appraising him, as though trying to figure out what they could take from him.

"Don't you look pretty and clean, Master," a soft voice said.

Patrick whirled. A dark shape rose from the shadows five or ten meters away. It was a man, his face barely visible in the dark. The man moved toward Patrick with a slow, limping gait.

A limp! It turned Patrick's stomach. He'd never seen a real person with a limp. It had been thousands of years since medicine had been perfected to such a degree that broken limbs could be fixed in a matter of hours.

The man came out of the shadows. Other than the limp, it was clear he was large and powerfully built. There was something about the way he moved that frightened Patrick, something predatory, like a hyena or a wolf edging toward its prey.

Suddenly a shaft of light revealed the man's face. It was a horrible mass of scars, like a pile of red worms. He only had one eye.

"Help a sick man, would you, Master?" the man said.

Without intending to, Patrick gasped.

The man extended a large, gnarled hand toward Patrick. A terrible odor accompanied him, like the scent of a rotting deer Patrick had once smelled when he went on a camping trip out West.

"I'm sorry, I—" Patrick stumbled backward, hitting the ground with an impact that shot through his entire body like a lightning bolt. "I must have made a mistake."

"I think you did, Master," the man said. His smile, a horrible twisted leer, split his face.

Patrick struggled to his feet. Every eye in the tunnel was on him. Laughter spread through the chamber, echoing eerily.

Patrick staggered backward, feeling for the handle of the huge iron door through which he'd just entered.

"Oh, you don't like us roaches, do you, Master?" the man said. "Well, maybe we don't like you so much either, hmm?"

Patrick's hand closed around the steel door handle. He wrenched it open and stumbled through the door. The big man dove toward him.

The last thing he saw before the big steel door slammed shut was a single bloodshot eye staring at him.

When Patrick stopped running, his chest felt as if it were encircled by bands of red-hot iron. He put his hands on his knees and tried to catch his breath. He felt light-headed, and his legs were trembling so hard he wasn't sure he was going to be able to remain standing.

"Hey," a voice said.

Patrick straightened up, his heart banging in his chest.

"You okay, friend?" A smiling man in a green jump-suit was looking at him inquiringly. Inscribed on his chest was a small sign that read MAINTENANCE—WE MAKE IT HAPPEN!

"I'm—fine," Patrick gasped.

"You sure?"

Patrick nodded.

"You're a little off the beaten path, aren't you?" the man said.

Patrick smiled weakly. "Thanks for your concern. I'm fine. Really."

"Okay," the man said dubiously.

After the man was gone, Patrick sat down and put his head between his knees. *I'm just not up to this*, he thought. *I've made a big mistake thinking that I had any business getting involved in a thing like this.*

Six

When Patrick got home, he slumped down in the chair in his living room and stared at the wall for a while. *Failure! Total failure!*

Everything had been working until he entered that tunnel. The prediction of which book would get stolen next. The tracking device. Following the thief. It was all perfect. Until he'd lost his nerve.

The man with the scarred face hadn't threatened him directly. He'd been a little rude. But that was all. *What it comes down to?* Patrick thought. *When the crunch came, I lost my nerve.*

Patrick wasn't even sure what he'd been afraid of. The dirt. The scars. The limp. The fires. The smoke. The strangeness of it all. He still couldn't believe that in this day and age people lived like that. Why? What were they doing down there? Cooking food with actual *fires*? It was bizarre.

Patrick sat for a long time, trying to think what he should do next. No one else would know that he had failed. In fact, everybody else seemed perfectly content to leave the matter to the detective from Unit 9. There were millions of books down there in the stacks underneath the public library. At this rate the thief could steal a book every day for the next thousand years and barely make a dent in the collection.

But it wasn't right! Once those books disappeared, they were gone forever. Sure, there were copies of them lurking someplace in the memory of a computer somewhere. But it wasn't the same as a real, physical book. The book that had been stolen was a signed first edition. It had actually been touched by L. Frank Baum over three thousand years ago.

Idly Patrick turned toward the far wall of his apartment. Right now it had an iridescent pattern moving around on it.

"Bring up my file of pictures from the ski trip I took to Colorado," he said.

Instantly the iridescent pattern disappeared, and the first of the security tapes appeared showing the cartoon character the thief used to mask his or her image during the first theft.

"Capture the image of the cartoon," he said. "Identify."

"The image mask is three-D model based on a hand-drawn cartoon," the voice of his computer said. "Based on color application and style, the original cartoon is probably twentieth century. Most likely before 1980."

"Can you do any better than that?"

There was a brief pause. "There is a ninety-seven percent likelihood that it is based on the work of Dr. Seuss."

"Who's he?"

"A children's book author and illustrator. Real name, Theodor Seuss Geisel, born March second, 1904, in Springfield, Massachusetts. Died—"

"Okay, okay," Patrick said. "Can you identify the specific character?"

There was a long pause. "Ninety-one percent likelihood the image is based on the Key-Slapping Slizzard of Solla Sollew."

"The *what*?"

By way of answer, the computer brought up the image of a book, along with a paragraph of information on the book and author. The title was *I Had Trouble in Getting to Solla Sollew*. Apparently this book was one of the lesser-known publications of the author known as Dr. Seuss. Patrick scanned the list of Dr. Seuss's most popular books. There was one book called *Green Eggs and Ham*. That sounded like an interesting one to read! Another time, perhaps. For now, Patrick scrolled through the text of *Solla Sollew*. It was about a furry creature who lived in an unpleasant place where he got stung and hit in the head. Tired of his life there, he decided to go to a perfect place called "Solla Sollew," a magical city where people didn't have problems. Unfortunately, when he got to Solla Sollew, there was a big wall around the town, and only one door in. And hiding in the lock of that door was a tiny mischievous critter that kept slapping away the keys of everyone who tried to enter. As a result, the furry creature had to go back where he came from. He went through all manner of crazy and difficult adventures. When he finally got home he realized that he didn't mind the place that much after all. The point of the story seemed to be that no matter where you go, there will always be problems.

"Huh," Patrick said, examining the illustration. "It's definitely the same character. Can you tell me anything else about it?"

"A little over a thousand years ago, when wars and crime were finally being stamped out by humanity, there was a movement that said humanity would always have problems. They took the Key-Slapping Slizzard as their symbol or mascot. They claimed that making a perfect society was a mistake, that humanity would be more vulnerable to bad things if everyone got out of the habit of struggling with evil and poverty and oppression."

"What happened to that movement?"

"They went underground. Literally. The people referred to as 'roaches' are their descendants."

"You mean they actually *chose* to be down there?"

"It was a long time ago."

"Speculate for me as to why somebody would have chosen this image to mask what they were doing."

"I'm not good at guessing, Patrick."

"Try it anyway."

"Possibly they are attempting to indicate their belief that our current way of life could all fall apart."

"That's kind of what I was thinking too."

"The Slizzard movement claimed that every society had the potential to hit a tipping point that would send it into a death spiral from which it couldn't easily recover."

"Like what?"

"It could be anything. A war between competing groups or nations. A failure of some kind of basic technology. Climate change. Crop failures. An energy source that disappeared."

"And they thought that could even happen to *us*?"

"Yes."

He stared at the hologram. The image of the Slizzard, two meters high, rotated slowly in front of him. It seemed to be watching him with its crazy-looking eyes.

If somebody had told him yesterday that the world could ever fall apart, he would have laughed at them. But there was something about those people down there in that tunnel that spooked him. There was no reason for them to live there. Food and shelter were free today. For whatever reason, the roaches *chose* to live down there. Dirty, hungry, sick, vulnerable to violence. It made no sense at all. And yet . . . there they were.

And if somebody could choose that . . . Well, what other terrible things could they choose?

"But why steal books? Why burn them? What's the connection? And why children's books?"

"I don't know, Patrick."

"Guess."

"I'm sorry. I cannot."

"What use are you then?"

"Actually, I am very good at—"

"Rhetorical question," Patrick interrupted.

"Oh."

How many thousands of years had they had computers? And they still couldn't give them a sense of humor.

After a moment a bell dinged, and the wall turned red.

"Your cat is missing," the computer said.

"No, it's not," Patrick said.

"Your cat is missing. Alert detected. Your cat is missing. Alert detected."

"Wait a minute, wait a minute!" Patrick said. "Where?"

A map appeared on the wall. It read PINE HAVEN WILDERNESS SITE.

"Here," the computer said.

"What is that?"

"It's a wilderness preserve one hundred and twelve kilometers north of your current location. It contains over forty miles of trails and a variety of wildlife, including thirty-four species of birds, three species of bats, elks, white-tailed deer, bison, cougars, wolves, red foxes, lynx, bobcats, coyotes—"

"Okay, okay, okay. But where's my . . . uh . . . cat?"

"Your cat has been detected in a cave six kilometers from the entrance to the park."

"Call an air taxi. I want to go there immediately."

"I'm sorry, Patrick. That's not possible."

"What do you mean it's not possible!"

"It's a restricted area."

"Restricted to what?"

"Tourism is not allowed. Due to its status as a wilderness preserve, it can only be accessed for educational purposes."

"Educational purposes?"

"Yes, Patrick."

Patrick thought for a long time. "You know what I think?" he said finally.

"No, Patrick."

"Time for a field trip!"

SEVEN

The class arrived at the wilderness preserve early the next morning and disembarked from the bus. As soon as they had unloaded their packs full of gear, the bus sped away.

Patrick had realized that a field trip to the preserve was actually the perfect answer. First, by bringing his class in the guise of an "educational field trip," he would be granted access to the park so that he could recover the stolen book. But even more important, he would have the entire class with him. He hoped that during the course of the field trip, he would be able to figure out who had been to the park before, and that would tell him who had stolen the book. Besides, it would be a nice break for the rest of the students to have some time outside. Often people grew so accustomed to the pace of daily life underground that they stopped coming above the surface to enjoy the beauty to behold there. As far as Patrick was concerned, reminding his students of life up here was a helpful lesson for them.

"Okay, everyone," Patrick said as soon as each of his students had shouldered their packs. "I want you to listen carefully." The group was huddled in the chilly morning air next to a small wooden shelter at the edge of the road. "We spend most of our time underground. Some of you might feel a little uncomfortable with all the open space. That's okay. In fact, it's a good thing. You need to stay sharp here. This is a wilderness preserve. Em, I asked you to do a little research. Would you be so kind as to tell us about the animals that live here?"

Em stepped forward, brushed her short blond hair back from her forehead. "The preserve contains eleven cougars, nine black bears, and two wolf packs. All these animals are capable of killing and eating humans. As a general rule they will stay away from a group of people. But wolves and cougars, in particular, have no problem attacking and killing individual humans. Four years ago, a doctoral student was killed and eaten by a cougar. All they found was her pinkie finger."

A chorus of voices murmured surprise and excitement.

"In addition," Patrick added, "we'll be crossing a number of streams. The forecast today is for pop-up thunderstorms. A small stream can suddenly turn into a flash flood. There are several high promontories that—"

"What's a promontory?" one of the students, a boy named Roger, said.

"A cliff," Jay Oh said, rolling his eyes.

"Hey, everybody here isn't a genius!" Roger said.

"Two boys snuck in here last year and fell off some

high rocks," Patrick added. "I wouldn't even call it a cliff. It was only four meters high. But one of the boys died before help arrived."

"Any other cool fatalities here?" Jay said.

Patrick frowned at him. "Look, you can joke all you want. But this is not your snug little tunnel back home. There are an enormous number of things that can go wrong here. Hypothermia, lightning, trees falling on you, slipping and falling, animal attacks, I mean the list goes on and on. So don't get separated from the group. And when I ask you to do something, do it." He knew the likelihood of any real danger to the kids was minute as long as they were careful and followed common sense, but he figured the more he scared them, the safer bet that the students would indeed take care.

"Dr. Discipline!" Jay said.

"We've got comms, though, right?" Em said, holding up her silver communicator.

"Sure, of course. You've all got your comms. We can track all of you with them. If you run into trouble or get separated from the group, give me a shout on the comm, and I'll come find you."

"So . . . remind me, why are we doing this?" a student named Shana asked. She was a tall, athletic girl who, if anything, was even more rebellious than Jay Oh.

"Education," Patrick said.

Shana looked at Jay and made a face. Jay laughed.

"All right, let's go," Patrick said.

Twenty minutes later it began to rain.

Shana looked up incredulously at the sky. "Wow,"

she said, holding out her hands, letting the fat drops smack against her hands. "It feels funny doesn't it?"

It wasn't that the kids had never been aboveground. But very few people spent much time outside. And if they did, they certainly didn't stand around in the rain. She stared up at the angry sky. Wet drops of rain splashed onto her face. Then she began to look fearful. "Are we going to get struck by lightning?"

"Highly unlikely," Patrick said. "There are two trails. The short trail goes over that ridge over there." He pointed at a large hill topped by bare rock. "I was planning on taking the short trail. But I think you're right. It wouldn't be much fun if we got struck by lightning. We'll take the long trail. We should be okay."

"You sure?" Jay Oh said, a note of challenge in his voice.

"Sure," Patrick said. He wished he felt as sure as he sounded, though. He was an experienced hiker, but thunderstorms still scared him. The boiling clouds above the group looked like a cauldron of gray fire.

The novelty of the rain wore off quickly. Soon it was just uncomfortable and cold. The students grumbled as they filed down the path through the ancient trees.

"Why can't we go back?" Shana said.

"Yeah!" said Roger. "This stinks."

"The bus won't be back until nightfall," Patrick said. "We'd just be standing there in the rain."

The grumbling continued as the rain continued to fall.

"How did people stand it before we lived underground?" one of the students said.

"People were different back then," said another student. "They didn't feel things the way we do."

"Not true," Patrick said. "They just had to endure things we don't." He lifted the collar of his coat. It only served to funnel more rain down his neck. He decided to try distracting the kids. "Anyone care to name some things our ancestors had to put up with that we do not?"

"Cancer," said Em.

"Sunburn," said Roger.

"Heat and cold."

"War."

"Crime."

"Good," Patrick said. "Anything else?"

Patrick continued to ply them with questions, but after a while the group sank into a glum silence, refusing to answer.

Finally Shana said, "I'm done."

"Look, Shana——," Patrick said.

"Nope. Forget it. I'm going back. I'm getting on the comm and calling for an air taxi."

She pulled her comm off her belt, frowned, shook the comm. "Crud!" she said. "There's something wrong with my comm."

"Shana!"

But Patrick's headstrong student refused to listen. She simply turned and walked back down the sodden trail, talking angrily to her comm.

"Shana, you get back here right now, or you'll be repeating this class!" he shouted. He hated teachers who threatened things all the time. But he simply couldn't have kids wandering around in the woods by themselves.

Shana didn't even look back.

"Wait at the shelter, young lady," he shouted. "I'll deal with you when we get back!"

Shana disappeared around the bend.

Patrick pulled out his comm so he could track Shana. But strangely, his comm wasn't working right either. SIGNAL STRENGTH ZERO read the display. He'd never even *seen* a message like that on a comm before. Something must have happened to the satellite uplink. Underground there were low-frequency radio transmitters in every room and tunnel. But aboveground comms had to rely on satellite relays. If something happened to the satellite connection . . .

"That's strange," he said.

"You didn't hear?" Jay Oh said with an odd little smile. "Sunspots. It's messing up all aboveground communications satellites right now." He waved his comm in the air. "Mine's been offline since we left Manhattan."

Patrick felt a knot of fear in his gut. This was not good.

"Guess we all have to go back, huh?" Roger said hopefully.

Patrick clamped his jaw shut. "No. She can go back and wait in the shelter until we get there."

"Oh, because the rest of us are just *loving* standing out in the rain," Roger said.

Jay Oh eyed Patrick with a cryptic smile on his face, as though he were watching an interesting science experiment.

"What are you grinning at?" Patrick said, snapping

uncharacteristically at the boy. He turned and began walking down the trail. "Let's move!"

The mood of the class worsened with every stride. *Am I doing the right thing?* Patrick kept thinking. The book might not even be in the cave. It might be a decoy signal. The thief might have found it and hidden it there. It might be anything.

And even if it really was in the cave, was it worth the risk to the students just to find it?

Oh, don't be ridiculous. It's not really dangerous. It's just uncomfortable. Kids today had it ridiculously easy, he reminded himself. A little discomfort would do them good, and he knew he could keep them safe.

As they continued to thread their way through the canopy of massive trees, Patrick tried to keep a close eye on the students to see if any of them showed any familiarity with the terrain. If the thief was among them, eventually he or she would likely give themselves away. But the students just plodded along listlessly, staring at the ground.

The rain continued for most of the morning. It was late spring and the temperature was relatively mild. But some of the students, used to the constant seventy-two-degree air underground, were starting to shiver.

"Why aren't we there yet?" Roger said. "I thought you said—"

"We took the longer trail to stay off that exposed ridge," Patrick said. "I guess it's taking a little longer than I thought."

But Patrick was worrying a little now too. It seemed it was taking a good bit longer than he'd expected. The trail had split several times. He had been confident each time that he'd taken the correct route. But now he wasn't so sure.

He had thought about bringing a map printed on plastic paper, but then he'd decided not to. The comm would work fine. Now that he was here, he found the tiny screen was hard to read. And without the satellite uplink to give them directions, he was beginning to suspect that he'd taken a wrong turn. Even the long trail was only supposed to have been eight kilometers. Surely they had traveled farther than that by now.

At around eleven thirty the rain finally ended, and the sun burst out from behind the clouds. As a shaft of warm light hit them, the students broke into a ragged cheer.

"See?" Patrick said. "This isn't so bad, huh?"

He decided now that they had a little good news, maybe he'd better break the bad news to them.

"That said, without the satellite uplink, I think I may have, uh . . ."

There was a loud groan from the group.

"You're saying we're *lost*?" one of the students said.

"We're not lost. We just . . . went a little out of the way," he said. He pointed to the gentle incline rising up from the trail. "Jay and Em, I want you guys to climb up this hill. Look around in all directions until you spot a small lake. That's where we're heading. We'll just figure out a way to get there. Okay?"

Jay and Em shrugged, looked at each other, then began trudging up the hill.

As he watched them go, Patrick studied Jay carefully.

Did he show any signs of having been here before? As far as Patrick could tell, he was basically a good kid. But he was also one of those people who resisted authority at every turn. Plus, he was one of the brightest students Patrick had ever had. Whoever had stolen the books had also done some very high-level trickery on the computer to hide what he'd done. Most of the students in the class just didn't seem to have the mental horsepower to do what this thief had done.

His gaze shifted to Em. She might well have been even smarter than Jay. But she wasn't a rebel. He just didn't see her as the type to destroy irreplaceable historical artifacts.

Patrick sighed. If either Em or Jay had been here before, they showed no sign of it.

"What do you think, guys?" Patrick said. "Lunch break?"

While the students perched themselves on a fallen log and began pulling out their lunches, Patrick pulled out his comm again. It was still not working correctly. Then, for a moment, the satellite link strengthened, and he could see the route they should have taken on the tiny map. They were about two kilometers off the trail. There had been a fork, and he'd taken the wrong path. He remembered it clearly and saw his mistake now. Fortunately, it would be easy to get back.

He quickly checked the tracer to see if he could tell where Shana was. He was glad to see that the tiny red circle representing her location showed up brightly on the map. But then—to his dismay—he realized that she wasn't anywhere close to the shelter by the road. Instead, she was on completely the wrong trail. He zoomed in on her location. The trail she was on, he noticed, actually put her closer to the cave than Patrick and the rest of the class were. He frowned. Why hadn't she gone back to the shelter? Was she lost? This whole thing was going from bad to worse. Then he noticed shading on the area where Shana was apparently hiking. He could just make out an overlay on the shaded area that read WOLF PACK RANGE. DO NOT ENTER WITHOUT SUPERVISION.

This was not good. Wolves were actually the most effective predators on the American continent. A wolf pack could take down a lone human without even breaking a sweat.

As he was staring at the tiny screen, the red circle wavered and disappeared. DOWNLINK FAILED. SIGNAL STRENGTH ZERO.

Patrick swallowed.

"Em!" he yelled, cupping his hands around his mouth. "Jay! Guys! Get back down here. Now!"

There was no answer.

Suddenly Patrick felt his heart beating and his palms sweating. This was bad. This was really bad.

"Are you okay, Patrick?" one of the students, Casey, said.

"I'm fine," he said. "I just need Em and Jay to get back here. My comm connected to the satellite for a minute. I know where we are now."

"I'll run up and get them," Casey said, smiling.

"Don't go too far," Patrick said.

Casey nodded and ran up the hill.

As he watched her disappear into the trees, something struck him. What if Shana had staged the whole blowup about the rain? What if she was heading for the cave on the shorter trail? Was it possible *she* was the book thief?

She certainly had the rebellious attitude. The question was, did she have the kind of mind that would dream up a crime like this? And if she did, could she have executed it? She was clever. But she just didn't seem the type. Whoever had staged the crime was trying to make a point. About what, Patrick hadn't yet figured out. But this was more than just random vandalism.

Or . . . was it? Maybe this was just a case of an angry teenager taking out her anger by destroying something valuable.

While he was thinking, Casey came running back down the hill breathlessly. "Em fell!" she called. "Em fell!"

"What do you mean, she fell?" Patrick said, snapping out of his thoughts.

"She did something to her ankle. Maybe even broke it!"

"Okay, everybody," Patrick called. "We're all going up the hill."

"I haven't finished my lunch yet," Roger protested.

"Eat while you hike," Patrick said. He clapped his hands. "Let's go!"

Em was lying in a bare gray outcropping of rock at the top of the small ridge. Her face was twisted with pain. Her pants were red with blood. Jay sat next to her, holding her hand.

As soon as he saw Patrick, he looked up accusingly. "Where *were* you? I called and called!"

Patrick shook his head. "I'm sorry! We couldn't hear you." He ran over and knelt next to Em. "What happened?"

She took a deep, shuddering breath. "I went up on that rock. To see what was around us. Otherwise the view is blocked. By the trees."

"She slipped and cut her leg," Jay said. "She may have even broken her ankle."

Patrick looked around at the somber group of students. "Is anybody's comm working? We need to call for an air ambulance."

Everyone pulled out their silver communicators, stared at the screens. Then everyone shook their heads.

"Okay," Patrick said. For a moment he felt panic welling up inside. But then, to his surprise, his mind went calm, and he began thinking clearly. "Okay, we're going to have to make a device they used a long time ago. It's called a 'stretcher.' Roger, Casey, go get some sticks. Four centimeters thick, two and a half meters long. Jay, Ken, I'll need your coats."

Within ten minutes they were heading down the hill, one student supporting each corner of the makeshift stretcher formed by threading pine poles through several coats.

"I'm sorry, Em," Patrick said.

Em gave him an odd look. "Well, I can't say this won't be a memorable trip, anyway," she said. She laughed briefly, then winced.

The group headed back down the trail. It didn't seem

to take them very long before they were back on the correct trail again. A small sign pointed in the direction of the shelter.

Patrick headed in the other direction.

"The shelter's this way," Jay said.

"I know," Patrick said. "But we're not going that way."

Everyone's eyes widened. "But we have to get medical attention for her."

"Well," Patrick said, "we've got another problem. . . ."

"What?" Jay said angrily.

In the distance a high, eerie howl cut through the silence of the forest. Patrick felt the hair stand up on the back of his neck.

"Wolves," Patrick said.

EiGHt

Once Patrick had explained about Shana going into the area where the wolves were, Jay said, "Why don't we split up? Four of us can take Em back to the shelter and—"

"Wolves can smell blood from more than three kilometers away. If the smell of Em's injury attracts them, I want us to have the largest possible group to fend them off."

"Yeah, but—"

Patrick shook his head. "We're not separating again. That's final."

He wasn't at all sure this was the right decision. At the speed they were moving carrying Em, he was not completely sure they'd be able to get to Shana and then get back to the shelter by nightfall. Part of him wasn't sure at all that he was making a good decision. Em's leg was still bleeding, and she needed medical attention. But he also knew that the worst thing he could do at this moment was to show uncertainty. He was the leader. The kids needed to feel confidence in him. If he wavered, they'd see it. And that would lead to more problems.

"Follow me," Patrick said. He began heading up the path. According to the map on his comm, which had been working again briefly, the trail he was on would meet up with the trail Shana was apparently following. And by happy coincidence, that would happen only half a kilometer from the cave that was his real destination on this trip.

For a moment no one moved.

"Follow me," Patrick said again. Then he turned his back on the students.

What if they don't follow me? he thought. There was really nothing he could do to force them. For a moment he felt as if he couldn't breathe. He had no choice but to go after Shana. If the kids didn't follow him, he'd have to do it alone.

Patrick was dying to look back. But he knew he'd look weak if he did. Sweat broke out on his skin. *Please follow me,* he thought. *Please!*

Then, just when he thought he'd lost them, Em's soft voice spoke. "He's right, guys. Splitting up's a bad idea. Let's go."

For a moment, nothing. Patrick felt his blood pounding in his ears.

Then, as if they were all of one mind, he heard the rustling of feet. They were following him.

Whew! That was close.

The group walked in silence after that. Occasionally they stopped and switched stretcher bearers. Everyone's hands were getting chafed raw. But nobody complained.

The sun had come out and small puffy clouds floated

in a bright blue sky. A gentle wind blew through the trees, cooling everyone just enough so that they didn't get overheated. It had turned into a perfect day.

Still, Patrick couldn't help feeling like a fool. All this over a book.

Every now and then he would cup his hands and call, "Shana! Hey, Shana! We're coming for you!"

Occasionally the wolves would howl. Each time they seemed closer.

The group's progress was painfully slow. Patrick looked up at the sun now and then. Underground it didn't matter what time it was. The lights were on all the time. But aboveground the world still moved to the ancient rhythms. Sunrise, sunset. Rain, wind, flood, drought, winter, spring, summer, fall. Once these things had been matters of life and death to people. Now they were just figures of speech.

Except . . . not up here.

The sun had been high in the sky when they had found Em lying on the rocky ridge. But now it was getting lower, obscured by trees. The world hadn't exactly gotten dark yet. But Patrick could sense the light subtly changing. The bright, optimistic light of midday was becoming paler, bleaker.

Getting out of the park by nightfall was starting to seem unlikely. They had no tents, no extra food or water, no shelter, no fire.

They reached the junction between the short trail and the long trail at four o'clock.

"Which way?" Jay said.

Patrick looked around. The short trail led toward

the wolves. The long trail went back they way they had come. But there was a third trail—the one that led to the cave.

Patrick pulled his comm off his belt and stared at it for about the fiftieth time. There was still no satellite signal. He took a deep breath. What was the right move? With no knowledge of where Shana was, there was no knowing which direction he ought to go. If he took the short trail, there was at least a distant chance that they could make it back to the shelter in time to catch the shuttle back to Manhattan. But if Shana had taken the spur that led off toward the cave, she'd be stuck out here all night. Alone. Unprotected.

Think! Think!

"Mr. Mac?" Alana said.

"Mr. Mac?" Roger said. "What are we going to do?"

"Mr. Mac, Mr. Mac, Mr. Mac—"

Suddenly everyone was talking. Patrick felt as if his head were in a vise.

"We need to go back, Mr. Mac," Roger said.

"Shana could be out that way!" Jay said, pointing down the trail leading toward the cave. "We can't leave her here."

"Maybe we should split up," a third boy said.

"Yeah," Jay said. "Me and you and Roger could go to the cave and—"

"*I'm* not staying out here!" Roger said.

"My mom and dad will *panic* if we don't get back tonight," another voice said.

Everyone began arguing. Patrick felt powerless to stop them. There was simply no good decision here. *I'm not some ancient frontier adventurer!* Patrick thought hopelessly. *I'm a librarian. What do I know about this?* He knew he needed to make a decision, needed to show some confidence so the kids didn't lose hope. But he felt frozen.

And then something hit him. The cave. Jay had just said that they should go to the cave. But Patrick had never even mentioned the cave. So how did—

"Quiet, everybody!" Patrick said. The voices died out. Patrick cocked his head at Jay. "I never mentioned the cave."

Jay blinked. "Huh?"

"The cave. I never told any of you that we were going to the cave. How did you know about it?"

Jay looked confused. He shrugged. "I don't know. I guess it was on the map. I just thought—" He broke off and swallowed. "What? What are you looking at me like that for?"

Patrick felt an odd sense of triumph. It was Jay. It had to be. Just as he'd suspected from the very beginning.

The feeling of triumph quickly faded. At this moment it really didn't matter one bit who the thief was. Patrick looked off into the trees. The sun was getting lower, and the shadows on the ground seemed darker.

"Mr. Mac?" Roger said. "What are we going to do?"

Patrick didn't have an answer. He looked around at the young faces, staring eagerly at him, waiting for him to give them an answer that would make them feel safe, that would make them believe everything was okay.

"I'm sorry," he said softly. "I didn't—when I planned this—I didn't think . . ." His voice drifted off.

"Mr. Mac?" Jay said.

"I'm sorry."

There was a brief, uncomfortable silence.

"All of you. Em. Everybody. I'm sorry."

Em sat up on her stretcher and looked at him. Then, improbably, she smiled. "It's okay, Mr. Mac," she said. "You know what to do."

And just like that, he did. He knew exactly what they had to do.

"Um, Mr. Mac?" It was Jay talking.

"Okay." Patrick clapped his hands together decisively. "Here's what we're going to do."

"Mr. Mac?"

"Let me finish."

"Mr. Mac?" Jay was pointing at something.

"*What*, Jay?"

Jay didn't speak. He just kept pointing.

To the left of the trail was a long, rolling meadow full of pink and red flowers. At the top of the meadow was a small rise. Standing at the top of the little hill, silhouetted against the blue sky, was an animal. It stared intently at Patrick with unblinking yellow eyes.

A wolf.

"We're going to the cave," Patrick said. "All of us."

Nine

One wolf. Then two. Then five. Then more.

"This way," Patrick said firmly. "Girls, get the stretcher. Everybody else surrounds it. Jay, Roger, you're the biggest. I want you in the rear."

Four girls immediately hoisted Em and began walking briskly down the trail. At the far side of the meadow, the wolves began to move. The lead wolf was snow white. It crept toward them, head down, teeth slightly bared, sniffing the air.

"Eric," Patrick said sharply, "look for tree limbs on the ground. Two meters, no more than three centimeters thick. And they can't be rotten."

Patrick reached into his pack and pulled his camping knife out of its sheath. All potential weapons—even tools like chef's knives and camping knives—had been outlawed centuries ago. Strictly speaking, the knife was illegal. But every serious camper Patrick knew owned one.

Eyes widened at the sight of the gleaming knife.

"Sticks!" Patrick said, snapping his fingers urgently. "Now."

"What are the sticks for?" Eric said.

"Spears," Patrick said. "We're making spears."

At the rear of the group, Jay's face split into a broad grin. "Yeah!" he said. "Mr. *Mac*, coming through!"

Eric handed a small tree limb to Patrick. Patrick whacked it on a nearby tree. It cracked in half. "You've got to do better, Eric."

Eric nodded, darted into the trees. Patrick looked behind them. The wolves were in no hurry. They were trotting after the students, steadily closing the distance. *Maybe two hundred meters?* Patrick thought.

"Hurry, Eric!"

Moments later Eric burst out of the trees with several sticks. These were much better. Patrick quickly sharpened a point on the end of the first one, tossed it to Jay. A few quick strokes of his sharp blade and he had a second spear. He threw it to Roger.

"What do we do?" Roger said.

"If they get close, you kill them," Patrick said. He made a stabbing motion with the remaining stick. Then he turned to Eric. "More sticks."

Eric ran into the woods again.

Seeing that one of the group had separated, the wolves began picking up the pace, loping into the woods in the direction Eric had gone.

"Hurry, Eric!" Em called. "They're coming for you."

Eric didn't answer. Patrick could hear him tromping around in the brush. But he couldn't see him. There was thick foliage on the left side of the trail, blocking his view.

The white wolf was now only about seventy-five meters away.

"Eric," Patrick called. "Let's go. Time's running out."

Just as the white wolf burst into a run, Eric ran out of the trees, four more sticks in his hands. He was laughing and his eyes were wide.

He reached the group only seconds before the white wolf. As he did so, the wolf peeled off, circling back around to join the larger group.

The wolves now slowed, matching their pace to the students'. They weren't howling or growling, weren't making any noise at all. They simply shadowed Patrick and the students, heads lowered, eyes fixed on the humans.

Patrick furiously worked on the sticks, sharpening their points with his knife.

"Do you think Shana's all right?" one of the girls carrying Em said.

"If they're hunting us," he said, "they're hungry. If they're hungry, then they never . . ." He searched for the right word. Attacked? Ambushed? Ate? "If they're hungry, they never . . . uh . . . found Shana."

"I hadn't thought of that," the girl said, looking relieved.

Patrick hoped he was right.

"How much farther?" Jay said nervously. The wolves had formed a loose half circle around the students.

Now that he had finished making the spears, Patrick moved to the rear of the group. "Not far," he muttered.

The white wolf darted forward, lunging toward Patrick. Its hair bristled and its teeth were bared. Patrick jabbed furiously at the wolf. It darted this way and that, and he kept stabbing at it. He felt the spear bite. The wolf let out a shrill whimper and retreated.

"Yeah! Mr. Mac!" Roger shouted.

The wolves backed off a few meters. Patrick had a chance to count them now. There were seven adults and three smaller pups.

"Next one to get close," Patrick said, "the three of us need to jump out and really go after it. We need to show them who's boss. Otherwise they'll just keep nipping at us until one of us gets in trouble."

"They wouldn't *really* hurt us, would they?" Eric said.

Patrick had a long answer forming in his mind. He wanted to say that when you lived underground in Manhattan, you never felt unsafe for even a minute. There was no war, no crime, no danger of any sort. And if you did happen to stumble and bang your head, medical care was only minutes away. He wanted to say that only days ago, he too had felt that he lived in a world with no dark places, no threats, no danger, nothing at all to worry about. He wanted to say that his mind was beginning to change, that he was beginning to think that underneath the happy world they lived in, something dark was brewing.

But instead of giving Eric the long answer, Patrick just said, "Give them a chance, they'll take you by the throat, drag you down, and start eating you before you're even dead."

"Huh," Eric said, frowning. "Interesting." He scooped up a fist-size rock and hurled it at the wolves. The rock whacked a large gray male on the shoulder. It yelped in pain. "How you like that, wolfie, wolfie? Huh? You want to eat some more of that?"

A nervous burst of laughter rose from the group.

"Nice, Eric!" Patrick said. "Everybody grab some rocks and start thowing. That'll keep them back."

It was a standoff. For more than an hour the kids continued to hurl rocks as the wolves circled and probed, probed and circled. The wolves were wary of both the rocks and the spears. But they seemed to be adapting their tactics now, spreading out, probing in pairs and threes, so that Patrick and his students couldn't concentrate their fire on any single member of the pack.

The sun was getting lower and lower in the trees and the light started fading. Patrick felt sure they'd be safe in the cave. But if they got stuck out here in the open, in the dark, without fire . . . Well, it would be a long, long night.

And to make things worse, everyone was getting tired. They'd had to stop several times so the stretcher bearers could rest. And each time the wolves had gotten closer and more confident.

Suddenly a cry went up from one of the girls in the front of the group. "Mr. Mac!"

Patrick whirled.

"There!" the girl called. "See it?"

Not more than thirty meters away was a large black crevice in the rock. The cave! They'd made it.

As though sensing that their prey was about to escape, the wolves began to growl and dart closer. They seemed as if they were summoning their nerve for an all-out charge.

"Hurry!" Patrick shouted. The group surged toward the cavern's entrance.

As they were about to enter the cave, a figure rose up out of the darkness. The group pulled up short. For a moment the same thought ran through the entire group: a wolf.

But then Patrick realized it was a human figure. A girl, waving her arms furiously.

"Hey!" the girl yelled. There was a broad smile on her face, smudges of dirt on her cheeks. But she looked to be in fine spirits. "You guys found me!"

Patrick felt overwhelmed with relief. "Shana!"

"I got bored sitting around that stupid shelter. So I tried to come back and find you. Did I take the wrong trail?" Shana grinned brightly. "Anyway, Mr. Mac, I'm sorry if I got all weird on you this morning. I was in a bad mood, and I took it out on you."

"No problem," Patrick said.

Shana pointed over his shoulder. "Hey, look!" Her eyes were shining. "Wolves!"

"We kinda noticed," Jay said dryly.

"Ohhhhh," she said in a high voice, clapping her hands in excitement. "They're so cuuuuuuute!"

Ten

Patrick wasn't sure exactly what he'd expected. That the book would be sitting there in the middle of the cave waiting for him? Maybe.

If that was what he had expected, it didn't work out that way. The cave was not a large flat-floored room like you always saw in the vids. It was a slanted crease in the stone, no more than three or four feet wide. You couldn't stand upright in it. You had to lean your back on the slimy rock.

The only good thing was that there was no way for the wolf pack to attack them. It was too narrow for more than one animal to enter at a time. Those were bad odds for the wolves—and the wolves knew it. After a few minutes of trotting back and forth in front of the entrance, the wolves suddenly turned and slunk back into the forest. They obviously felt they'd wasted enough time on the humans and were ready to find something that would be easier to kill.

After the wolves disappeared, Roger said, "So should we head on back, Mr. Mac?"

Patrick shook his head. "It's already starting to get dark out there," he said. "There's no way we'd make it back to the shelter."

"Maybe we could go by flashlight," Roger said, pulling a bright flash out of his pack.

"Wolves see a lot better in the dark than we do," Patrick said. "We're just going to have to wait out the night here."

The students didn't say anything. But it was obvious they were disappointed. As Patrick was readying himself to give them a little pep talk, Em said, "Mr. Mac, can I talk to you for a minute?"

Patrick looked at her curiously.

"Back there," she said, pointing into the murky depths of the cave.

"I'm not sure it's a good idea," he said. "It's hard to see, and I wouldn't want you to fall again."

"I shined my flashlight back there," she said. "It looks like the space opens up a little." Without waiting for his assent, she began inching her way back through the crevice.

Patrick followed her dubiously, threading his way through the line of students. It took about ten minutes for them to go fifty or sixty meters deep into the cave. Em should have been in a lot of pain. But she didn't seem to notice.

Suddenly she stopped and waved her flashlight in front of her. Patrick's eyes widened. A huge sparkling cavern opened up in front of them. The walls and ceilings and even the floor seemed to be lined with jewels.

"Wow," he said. "You were right."

She looked at him for a moment. "I've been here before," she said.

Patrick blinked, then stared at her. "Follow me," she said. Then she leaped down about two meters.

"Your leg!" he said.

"It's fine," she said.

"You mean—" He broke off in the middle of the sentence.

"There's nothing wrong with my leg. The blood was made of syrup and red dye."

"You made those kids carry you all this way?"

She nodded. He studied her face. She looked the same as ever—serious, calm, earnest. There wasn't a sign of shame or mischievousness on her face, no sign that she had done anything wrong at all.

"Come on." She motioned him to follow her.

Against his better judgment he jumped down into the cavern. As he hit the floor, he saw that the "jewels" on the walls were actually beads of water that had condensed on the rock.

Em was already walking briskly through the cavern. "Wait!" he called. But she didn't stop. His confusion was turning to anger. "Em, what's this all about? Did you steal those books?"

She just kept walking.

He followed her through the cavern, into a narrow tunnel, then into a smaller chamber. This one was full of multicolored stalactites and stalagmites. It was brightly lit by a light source that Patrick couldn't see.

Strangely, a man stood in the middle of the room. Patrick did a double take.

"He did great, Press," Em said to the man as Patrick entered the room.

"Okay, who are you and what is this about?" Patrick demanded.

The man gave Patrick a big, disarming smile. "Hey, I'm sorry we put you through all this nonsense," the man said. "But it was for your own good."

Patrick looked at Em, then at the man whose name, apparently, was Press. "Do you have the book?"

"Oh, we've got all of them," the man said. He pointed to his left. Sitting in a neat stack were the stolen books.

"But—they were burned up!" Patrick said.

Press shrugged. "I guess if you can make it look like they were being stolen by a three-thousand-year-old cartoon, you could make it look like they were getting incinerated, too."

"We had the director's full consent and assistance," Em said. "Without her access codes, Jay would never have been able to rig the security vids."

"So, wait a minute . . . Jay was in on this too?"

Patrick heard laughter echoing behind him. He looked up to see Jay sitting on the lip of the path leading down into the cavern, his feet swinging lazily. "I'm Em's acolyte," he said.

Patrick was feeling more confused—and maybe even humiliated—by the moment. None of this made any sense at all.

"I'm sorry," he said, turning to the man who had been waiting for them in the cavern, "but exactly who are you?"

The man laughed genially. "That's a trickier question than you might think."

Em said, "Press and I are what's known as 'Travelers.' He's the Traveler from Second Earth and I'm the Traveler from Third Earth."

Patrick looked at them blankly.

"You've been lucky so far here on Third Earth," Press said. "So far Saint Dane has yet to operate here. But when he comes, we'll need to be ready. *You'll* need to be ready. You see, in some respects Third Earth is more vulnerable than any other territory in Halla. The people of Third Earth have nearly forgotten what life-and-death struggle is all about."

"Wait, wait, wait," Patrick said. "What is all this about travelers?"

Press frowned. "I'm sorry. I'm getting ahead of myself." Press looked at Patrick for a moment, scratched his face, then said, "I've got a lot to tell you. You might want to sit down. . . ."

After Press had finished the long explanation about Travelers and Halla and Saint Dane, Patrick said, "Okay, so assuming this isn't the world's most elaborate practical joke, why did you steal the books?"

"It's your destiny to be a Traveler," Press said. "But that doesn't mean you don't need a little push. Your confidence needed a jolt. Finding these books wasn't a test. Think of it as training. Preparation. Some Travelers are natural—I guess you call them— men of action. Or women of action. The Traveler from Zadaa—her name is Loor—she's ready to go at the drop of a hat. To prepare her, she needed to learn restraint. You, on the other hand, you needed to see that you have more courage, more strength, than you probably give yourself credit for. You needed to see what you were capable of."

"What *am* I capable of?" Patrick said skeptically.

"Look at what you did today. In the face of all kinds of danger, you managed to keep your group safe, and you recovered a hugely valuable artifact, something that's important both to you and to the world at large. And you did it with a lot of grace and good cheer. You didn't force those kids to do what they did. They actually had fun. They love you. That's a harder trick than you might think. Being a Traveler is not just about courage. It's about leadership. And that's what you demonstrated today."

Patrick felt something warm moving inside him. On the face of it this whole story seemed ridiculous. And yet there was something about it that felt familiar. It was like the feeling he had when he came back home after being on a long vacation. As though a part of him had been waiting for this all his life.

"Mission, Patrick," Press said. "Everybody needs a mission in life. This is yours."

Patrick took a deep breath. He didn't know quite how to feel. If what this man was saying was true, then it was very scary and very exciting at the same time.

"This is just the beginning, Patrick," Press said. "This is just the beginning." Press paused. Then his smile faded. "But I have to tell you, it's only going to get harder from here."

ELEVEN

The next day an emergency airlifter arrived and picked up the whole class. The students had slept on the floor of the cave that night, and everyone was looking stiff and bleary as they stepped onto the lifter.

Before they climbed on, Shana ran out of the cave and threw her arms around Patrick. "Thank you for taking us here, Mr. Mac!" she said. "This was the best day of my life! I'm going to remember this forever."

The whole group cheered. "Yeah, Mr. Mac! This was the best!"

Patrick looked around at the group, smiling and feeling a little stunned. He had expected them to be angry with him for getting them into this mess. But they weren't angry. They were grateful.

When they got on the plane, Em sat down next to him. She wore a large ring on her finger, with odd writing on the sides.

"Every Traveler has his or her own path to walk," she said. "My job was to get you ready to be a Traveler in your own right. My work is done."

Patrick nodded, still trying to make sense of all this in his head. "Why did you go into the tunnels under the city?" he asked. "How did you get out here?"

"The deepest tunnels in the city are connected to the intercity magtrain lines. I took the train up here. There's a maintenance stop underneath the caves and a maintenance tunnel connects right to it. So I came up inside the cave, placed the books, then went back down into the tunnels and took the magtrain home."

"Why all that trouble?"

"We knew you'd use the computer to predict the next book. Once we figured that out, we knew you'd put a tracer in it. Tracer signals can only go through a few feet of rock, so we had to go deep underground to break up the tracer signal. Then, once we came back up here, the books were close enough to the surface for a clean signal to get out."

"It seems like an awful lot of work."

"On most of the territories, the Travelers run into big challenges all the time. But here on Third Earth, nothing ever goes wrong. We had to be the Key-Slapping Slizzard, see? We had to keep you out of Solla Sollew for a little while."

As they were talking, Patrick's comm beeped. "I guess the sunspots must be over," he said.

The comm beeped again.

He thumbed the talk button and looked at the screen. It was Sergeant Lane, the Unit 9 detective.

"Hello, Pat," the detective said. "I just wanted to let you know that there's been another theft."

Patrick frowned. "What? That's not possible."

"What do you mean?"

"Well, I've been lying on the floor of a cave a hundred kilometers from New York all night. Every one of my students has been with me."

Sergeant Lane looked puzzled. "That's very odd," he said. "Very odd indeed. They used the same security codes." He shrugged. "Well, hey, I'm as puzzled as you are. But I just thought I'd call to let you know. I'm uploading the security vids to your comm. Take a look and see if you spot anything that might help me out."

"Okay." Patrick's comm beeped, signaling the vid feed had been received. "So what book was stolen?"

"Something called the"—Sergeant Lane frowned as if trying to recall something—"The Gutenberg Bible? Does that name ring a bell?"

Patrick's eyes widened. "But . . . that's one of the most important historical artifacts in the whole—"

The screen went blank before Patrick could finish talking.

He turned to Em. "Did you hear that?"

Her brow furrowed. "But it doesn't make sense. We were right here. Obviously we couldn't have . . ." Her voice broke off.

Patrick queued up the security vid and began running it. It showed the Key-Slapping Slizzard, same as before, dashing through the library, stealing a book, taking it out onto the front steps of the library and burning it.

Em's face was white. "This is not good."

Patrick felt something clutch in his chest. He replayed the final part of the vid. It was a little different from the earlier vids. This time the Slizzard dumped some kind of chemical on the book and ignited it. The entire book was consumed in seconds. It could have been a fake, too. But in retrospect, the fire in this vid looked much more convincing than it had in the other ones.

Patrick replayed it twice. There was an odd hitch in the vid, a sort of stutter in the image as the book ignited.

"Wait!" Em said. "What was that?"

"I was wondering that too," Patrick said.

He reran the vid, this time on slow speed. It happened again. One frame was different from all the others, as though something had flashed. It was still too quick to make out what it was.

"Stop!" Em said.

Patrick stopped the vid and began backing it up, frame by frame by frame. And suddenly there it was. One single frame was different from all the others. Instead of the Key-Slapping Slizzard, Patrick could see a flesh-and-blood human standing there, the Gutenberg Bible on the ground before him, a small flame extending from his hand.

It was an extremely tall man, staring toward the camera, with a broad smile on his face. He had pale blue eyes and long gray hair. And despite the fact that he was smiling, there was something vaguely menacing about him.

And then, as quickly as they had found the picture, it began to fade. As the image of the man faded, it was slowly replaced by the image of the Key-Slapping Slizzard. For a moment nothing was left of the man but his smile.

And then that too was gone.

"Who was that?" Patrick asked. "Do you think that was the person who really stole the book? Or was it just some random image that infected whatever program was used to generate the Slizzard?"

Em kept staring at the screen.

"Oh, no," she whispered finally. "There's even less time than we thought."

PENDRAGON

Bobby Pendragon is a seemingly normal fourteen-year-old boy. He has a family, a home, and a possible new girlfriend. But something happens to Bobby that changes his life forever.

HE IS CHOSEN TO DETERMINE
THE COURSE OF HUMAN EXISTENCE.

Pulled away from the comfort of his family and suburban home, Bobby is launched into the middle of an immense, interdimensional conflict. It's a journey of danger and discovery for Bobby, and his success or failure will do nothing less than determine the fate of the world. . . .

Coming Soon: Book Ten

From Aladdin Paperbacks • Published by Simon & Schuster

THE FINAL
PENDRAGON

IS COMING
MAY 2009

ARE YOU READY?

TELL US AT
THEPENDRAGONADVENTURE.COM

3 1901 05281 8673